THE HOMETOWN WEEKLY

Good News For a Change

HUMOROUS TALES FROM
PARLEY GROVE

THE HOMETOWN WEEKLY

Good News For a Change

HUMOROUS TALES FROM PARLEY GROVE

BRUCE LINDSAY

Covenant Communications, Inc.

Cover Image *Open for Business* © Emily Dubowski

Cover design copyrighted 2008 by Covenant Communications, Inc.

Published by Covenant Communications, Inc.
American Fork, Utah

Printed in Canada
First Printing: September 2008

15 14 13 12 11 10 09 08   10 9 8 7 6 5 4 3 2 1

ISBN-13 978-1-59811-600-7
ISBN-10 1-59811-600-2

For my wonderful parents, Richard and Marian,
who taught me to love my hometown.

ACKNOWLEDGMENTS

My thanks to Robert Armstrong, M.D., of Manti, Utah. His anecdote about a Sunbeam teacher's visit to a doctor—widely circulated on the Internet—was the seed from which sprouted the story "Sunbeams." It was adapted with his generous permission.

Also, thanks to my brother, Gordon Lindsay, for finding a parable in the perils of a Halloween night spent with two of his sons. His account and insight were the genesis for "The Pumpkin and the Pillowcase."

The other stories contain more autobiography than I can prudently disclose. Most of the characters in this collection grew out of people I knew and loved in my hometown. I have simply blended their essence with a little imagination. I am grateful to each of those good souls for being so wonderfully real. Surviving townsfolk, relatives, and old friends may try to guess whether there is something of them in these pages. That's the risk a writer takes.

My hope is that every reader will recognize at least some of these characters from his or her own experience. Please remember: the people in Parley Grove are all fictional—except for the ones you know personally.

You can find more background and comments on these stories at www.thehometownweekly.com.

—Bruce Lindsay

Naturally, if we don't think our hometown is the greatest in the world, we are not very loyal citizens. We all should feel that way.

Harry S. Truman
From the rear platform of his campaign train
September 21, 1948
American Fork, Utah

TABLE OF CONTENTS

"Good news" is out there for the asking. Turns out, you just need to know where to look. It's all there in *The Parley's Progress,* a little Utah hometown weekly newspaper—the *good news* newspaper that will help you remember who you are and where you're from.

Can teaching Sunbeams really land you in the psych unit? Just ask Iola Heugely, who narrowly escaped exactly that on a trip to visit her daughter Kaelynne in Las Vegas. That, and Ordell Bithel bearing his testimony in tongues . . .

Changes Announced in Church could mean lots of things—and you won't believe what happens when Stake President RDell C. Markum sets his sights on Cloby Stubsted. There's a trip to Richfield in it, for sure . . . not to mention a name change for Cloby.

It's about time NonaRene Nelford got a new car—and *not* a truck or a station wagon, either—but little does she know that when she and LaEarl head up to Salt Lake to buy one, that pistol in her purse could be more trouble than she bargained for.

You're sure to recognize the characters slated for this year's Mother's Day program . . . and there's not a mom out there who won't relate to Vertis Euler's desire to have *all* her kids—even Destry!— home for Mother's Day.

Svena Oleson chose the worst possible time to die, and now Relief Society President Ralphene Hedberg has to juggle a funeral and a wedding lunch—for her very own daughter, Charnelle—at the same time . . . and in the same building!

Cloby Stubsted is taking his new calling *very* seriously—so seriously that he's willing to do just about *anything* to get that envelope back from Postmistress Effel Tolley. But Effel takes *her* job very seriously, too, and she's not giving in.

Arzley Criddle's obituary only tells *part* of the story (but then, don't they all?). Find out what happened when Elder J. Golden Kimball shared a room with him at Uncle Varno's in Richfield—and how love truly *is* blind.

When BreeAnn Ovard auctions off the five-month-old Columbia lamb she had as her 4-H project, Vern Hundrup ends up being *very* sorry that he talked Amber—with her double-dark-creamy-peanut-butter-tan—into leaving California . . .

When Bishop Leland D. Thaxton's brother Kayden comes from Alpine for the deer hunt, the kindly bishop discovers a mean streak of sibling rivalry—compounded by a pillowcase full of candy, a Richard Nixon mask, and a pumpkin-toting three-year-old in a *Finding Nemo* costume.

When seventy-eight-year-old Belwin Norby announces he's retiring as Taylor County surveyor, it's up to the men down to VarDell's Barbershop to find a suitable replacement. Seems like a slam-dunk when they find out that part-time seminary teacher Ethan Fitzpatrick is the only other surveyor in the county . . . but things are seldom as easy as they seem!

When TV reporter Hunter Rage happens upon a wall of smoke and flame at the edge of Parley Grove, she calls the Channel Eight Frenzied News Live at Five team with the promise of an exclusive. Wait until you see how *The Progress* covers the same event . . .

INTRODUCTION

Everybody has to figure out how to put food on the table, and I've been doing it as a television newscaster for a long time now.

During that time, more people than I could count have asked me essentially the same question. They've asked it on the street, at the grocery store, on the bus, at the barbershop, and at schools. They've even asked it on the phone.

The question everyone asks goes something like this: "Why don't you give us some good news for a change?"

If I had a dime for every time I've been asked that question, I think I could retire.

I'm not here to debate the state of journalism. That's a good topic, and we ought to talk about it.

But not right now.

Right *now*, I'm just here to oblige all those people who asked the question.

I'm here to give them, and give you, some good news—*and nothing but good news*—for a change. Turns out, you just have to know where to find it. And I think I *have* found it in a little Utah hometown weekly newspaper—the *good news* newspaper that will help you remember who you are and where you're from.

THE
PARLEY'S PROGRESS

SERVING PARLEY GROVE, UTAH'S 87TH LARGEST CITY, AND ALL OF TAYLOR COUNTY

SUNBEAMS

The hometown weekly just came in the mail. The big headline this week:

TARs Officers Elected at PGHS

And below the headline is a three-column picture of four handsome kids from up to the high school who just got elected to be next year's TARs officers. The TARs is one of the biggest, most popular clubs at Parley Grove High School, right up there with the Rodeo Club, and the FFA, and the Parlettes Drill Team.

The story says:

Elected president was Kade Thackerall, son of DeVere and RoWayne Thackerall, grandson of David and Mavaleen Thackerall and Wayne and Rowanna Streeper, all of Parley Grove.

Chosen as vice-president was Tafton Wyntch, son of LaVerd and Shellon Wyntch, grandson of Garneal and Verda Wyntch and Varlo and Sherma Belcher.

Named as secretary was Apaysha Hedberg, daughter of Kanyon and Ralphene Hedberg, granddaughter

of Teancum and Arvilla Hedberg of Parley Grove, and Ralph and Vardis Plot of Spanish Fork.

Designated treasurer was Jilane Nelford, daughter of LaRon and Nelladee Nelford, granddaughter of LaEarl and NonaRene Nelford and Delbert and Rella Thaxton, all of Parley Grove.

That's the lineup for next year's officers of the TARs—the Teen-Age Republicans.

You can see *The Progress* knows how to market to the masses. The trick is to get as many names of your readers into the paper as you possibly can.

Which is why most people turn straight to "Out 'N About" by EvaDean Thiede, on page two. Call it the society page or the gossip column or whatever you will, it's the most popular feature in the weekly because it's got the most names in it on a regular basis. And *The Progress* pays EvaDean $12 a week to write it . . . like this:

OUT 'N ABOUT
By EvaDean Thiede

The frost caught up with us for two nights last week, but at least we got to see and smell the lilacs this year.

EvaDean generally starts out with something poetic like that, and then she moves right into her hard lead:

Among those standing last Sunday in the Parley Grove First Ward to share testimony were Rayston Jepperson, VaNiece Urmson, Ermalita

**Perkley, Thorellen Plott, and Ordell
Bithel, who gave his remarks in
another tongue.**

Now it may *be* that angels above us are silent notes taking. But in Parley Grove, angels can be the *least* of your worries. Because EvaDean's taking notes down here below, and she prints 'em in the weekly for all the world to read!

By the way, that other tongue—the other language Ordell spoke in—was Portuguese, they think. They think it's Portuguese, mostly because that's what Ordell thinks it was. Ordell was a missionary in Brazil about forty-eight years ago, which was long before the days of language training. But he "done his best with it," as he says, and likes to keep in practice. Once a month. So they're used to it in the Parley Grove First Ward. In fact, some of the kids on the back row—they shouldn't, but they do—say it right along with Ordell, every month, by heart. And maybe with a better accent. But that's the kind of news that makes the hometown weekly.

With the weekly, you don't keep a lot of secrets in Parley Grove. I don't mean that EvaDean ever prints the *real* juicy stuff, or ever even *hears* much of it, because Parley Grovers are a modest people. They don't go and blab all about their private business the way people do these days on TV. So EvaDean writes things like:

**Visiting from Parley Grove with
the family of Brock and Kaelynne
Lambert in Las Vegas last week was
Iola Heugely. Kaelynne is Iola's baby
sister and hails from Parley Grove,
both daughters of Demmett and
Laweena Heugely. Iola says one day
they all drove up to Mount Charleston
to get away from the heat, and a good
time was had by all.**

Which is exactly what Iola told EvaDean when she called her on the phone last Wednesday. (You see, any time Parley Grovers travel someplace farther than, oh, about Richfield—or just *to* Richfield—

they're expected to report in to EvaDean when they get back so it can make the paper.)

So Iola told EvaDean about her trip to Las Vegas. And EvaDean wrote it down. Now, EvaDean does not ask follow-up questions. She does not probe. Which is the way to be polite as a reporter, and which helped make for good news in this case, because Iola didn't want the world to know she spent half her trip to Las Vegas in the hospital.

Dr. Barney at the Parley Grove Medical Clinic has been warning Iola about her cholesterol and her blood pressure. And last year he said he was going to put her on some prescriptions. But first, he gave her three months to lose fifteen pounds, he said, to see if *that* might point to the root of her problem—and he said it with just about that much tact.

Well, Iola thinks her real problem is stress, with her job as the cook down to the senior citizens' center, and with her DUP lessons and the quilting club and all. Especially now, with teaching a Primary class every Sunday.

Bishop Thaxton called her in six months ago to get her to be more "churchy," as Iola says. He called her to teach the Sunbeams, the three- and four-year-old kids, who are a handful for an old maid in her fifties, no matter how much she says she loves children. And Iola hasn't been all that churchy most of her life. And those little kids, after six months, are just wearing this poor woman out and driving her to exasperation. Iola felt like she needed that Las Vegas vacation with at least one Sunday away from the Sunbeams. She needed it and she *deserved* it. So she got Chlorine Stubsted to be her substitute. And on Friday morning of Memorial Day weekend, Iola got into her Olds Cutlass and drove to Las Vegas to see her sister Kaelynne and to play Aunt Iola to Kaelynne's kids. They are mostly older than the Sunbeams, and usually pretty well behaved. And Iola likes to spoil 'em.

Before she left, Iola stopped by the ChatNChew Cafe to pick up two fresh, hot, world-famous ParleyBerry Pies to take to Kaelynne. ParleyBerry Pie is the thing a person from Parley Grove would miss the most in living away from home. She put the pies in the trunk and was on her way.

But getting to Las Vegas last week was not an easy trip. No air conditioning in the old Olds Cutlass, and Iola's radio doesn't work. And it was exceptionally hot in the desert for the last of May. And Iola was tired—tired in general, and tired especially because she had not slept well the night before. In fact, she'd had a terrible night.

Iola had dreamed she was teaching the Sunbeam class the lesson "I Am Thankful for My Hands." And in her dream, as those little Sunbeam kids looked at their hands, their hands got bigger and bigger. Then the *kids* got bigger and bigger. They sprouted like beanstalks and grew right through the ceiling. They towered over Iola. They picked up the little chairs in their hands and crushed them to pieces. They pulled the curtains off the window and tied Iola up, with her hands behind her back and a gag in her mouth. They carried Iola out the door, out of town, and over a bridge, where they tied her to a railroad track she never knew was there. Then they left her.

Iola heard a train whistle. Then she heard the locomotive and felt the vibration in the tracks. And around the bend came the train, speeding toward her. She looked up, and in the final instant, her eyes met those of the engineer. He was Bishop Leland D. Thaxton.

Iola woke up in a cold sweat. Her heart was racing and her head hurt. She was out of breath, and she felt *so bad.* She felt bad because she knew that her dream was telling her that she was running away from her call to teach and love the Sunbeams. And she felt *so bad* about it. She started to feel guilty for leaving them, guilty knowing that she was running away.

Iola sank lower and lower, until she wallowed in that guilt—and only *then* did she start to feel a little better, because guilt brings Iola such consolation. Feeling guilty makes her feel like she is *doing* something about a problem. And that made her feel a little better. It works every time. Iola is one of those people who thrive on guilt. It's a great energizer. For a lot of people in Parley Grove, guilt is about the most exciting sensation in their near-sinless lives.

So she was tired before she started the trip. Tired and worn out and worked up and guilty and fearful of the way those semis whizzed past on the freeway—*vroom, vroom*—like meteors. *They* were not good for Iola's blood pressure. Not good at all. By the time she pulled off the freeway in Mesquite, the car was overheating. The car was overheated and Iola was overheated.

The man at the station topped off her radiator with antifreeze at $8 a quart. He sold her a new air filter for $49 and sold her a quart of oil—a *special* motor oil that, for $23 a quart, would keep her tires from overheating. The trip was turning out to be more expensive than Iola had planned, but she was relieved to know she would be safe.

She found the vending machines in the service station and bought a Moon Pie, a package of Zingers, and two cans of root beer—one can to wash down the last of the potato salad she had packed in the Tupperware bowl with the cold bratwurst, and the other can of root beer for the road, through the desert, after the Moon Pie and the Zingers for dessert.

Well, it was a long drive with no air conditioning and no radio and the Cutlass topping out at fifty-nine miles an hour. So Iola started singing trip songs to keep herself company. She sang "I've Been Working on the Railroad."

She sang "Bill Grogan's Goat," until it reminded her of her dream in which she was tied to the railroad tracks. She sang "There Once Was a Lady Who Swallowed a Fly" and "Home on the Range." She sang "The Bear Went over the Mountain" and "She'll Be Comin' 'Round the Mountain"—all those wonderful old stupid songs you only sing around campfires or on long boring car trips, and nowhere else.

Iola started playing around with the some of the words. She made them about her.

She'll be driving her Olds Cutlass
Oh, my heck! That car is gutless,
She'll be driving her Olds Cutlass
When she comes.

Iola sang all the trip songs and still had nearly an hour to go, so she started in on songs she sang with the Sunbeams in Primary.

She sang "Give, Said the Little Stream" and "I Have Two Little Hands." She only sang that one partway through because it made her think of the dream. She sang "Jesus Wants Me For a Sunbeam," and she changed that one a little bit, too:

The Sunbeams, the Sunbeams,
I'll teach *the Sunbeams for Him.*

Iola sang it for penance. She knew the Sunbeams were her cross to bear.

She was all sung out by the time she made it to Las Vegas. And then she took the wrong exit on the new freeway and didn't find her way to the Lamberts' driveway until it was nearly time for dinner.

The temperature was 108. Iola was exhausted. But all the kids came running out to meet her, and they all came out to greet her and to see if she had brought them anything—which, fortunately, she *had*. And they came to tell her all about soccer and dance lessons and the new doll and the stitches and the dead goldfish—everything they'd been storing up for a *week* to tell their Aunt Iola. All five of them were talking at the same time—they were going to *smother* her! She thought she would suffocate. But Kaelynne brought her a cold lemonade and had her sit under the patio cover next to the pool for the backyard barbecue in her honor.

Eating made Iola feel a little better. She loves barbecued ribs. And Iola had brought the dessert: those two ParleyBerry Pies—*world-famous* ParleyBerry Pies made fresh that morning at the ChatNChew. They did not have to reheat them. After crossing the desert in the trunk, the pies were hot enough. Kaelynne got out vanilla ice cream, and they all ate ParleyBerry Pie a la mode. The second helpings made Iola feel even a little better yet.

As the sun was going down, all the Lamberts and Aunt Iola climbed into the Suburban and drove over to the temple to let Iola see it all lit up so beautiful. They got out and walked around the grounds awhile and looked at the flowers and looked at the cactus, and Iola said again that she just couldn't get over how there can be something so wonderful and so beautiful in such a wicked place as Las Vegas.

When they got back in the Suburban, Brock told her that if you stay away from the Strip and from the casinos—as they do, of course—Las Vegas is a pretty nice community. Iola wasn't going to get into an argument about it, but she knew a lot of people from Parley Grove who aren't as well traveled as *she* is and who would find *that* pretty hard to believe.

Brock said the only time the family even *goes* to the Strip is when they take the older ones to ride the roller coaster at New York, New York.

A couple of the kids overheard that, and one of 'em said, "Oh Daddy, are we going to ride the roller coaster again?"

And another said, "Tonight?" And another one said, "I'm old enough to go." And another one said, "Can Aunt Iola come?" And another, "It's my very most favorite thing in the world, Daddy. Let Aunt Iola come and ride the roller coaster with us." And they all chimed in, "Oh, please, Daddy, please."

Well, you know where this was going. They *were* out to show Iola a good time. And she *is* a sport. It was only 9:30 and they could all sleep in tomorrow. And Brock *did* have ride passes left over from his meeting last week with his pharmaceutical reps. So this adventure was just bound to happen.

They drove the back way in to New York, New York, to avoid the Strip. It was a long walk from the car to the line for the ride, and it was still 102 degrees outside. Iola was out of breath by the time they got there, and again feeling a little faint, but there they were, face-to-face with the Manhattan Express—almost a mile of thrills on steel, with a 144-foot drop, two inversions, a vertical loop, and a Heartline Twist and Drop.

Iola, who *is* a sport, told herself that the wind on her face probably would make her feel better after such a stressful day.

Tafton, the youngest Lambert, was too small to ride, so Kaelynne stayed back with him. The rest of the kids and their dad and Iola paired up for the cars. Iola sat with the next youngest—the one who would fit in the seat with her.

The bar came down to lock them in the seats; the hydraulic brake released with a "whoosh," and they were on their way—heading up and up and up, higher and higher over the Las Vegas Strip. Iola was okay with the up and up and up part until she started thinking about the down and down and down. No wind yet on the uphill to cool her. In fact, she felt hotter than ever, as the Manhattan Express reached the summit to begin its dive, its 144-foot dive . . . 144 feet! That looked as tall as a mountain: 144 feet, nearly straight down, 144 feet at 67 miles an hour that feels like *600 miles an hour*. . . .

And just as they started to drop, Iola—who *is* trying to be more churchy—remembered she'd forgotten that morning to say her prayers! Just when she was getting into the habit. So she started to say one on the way down, a prayer that was mostly a promise to the Lord: if He'd get her out of this alive, she'd go back to Parley Grove and she'd be the best Sunbeam teacher there ever was, and she would not forget to say her prayers ever again.

Iola doesn't know if she ever finished that prayer. And she didn't remember the vertical loop or the Heartline Twist and Drop. When she opened her eyes again, she was under the examination lights at Sunrise Hospital.

Her EKG was normal. Blood sugar was within range. No trace of prohibited drugs in her system. (The drug test on Iola was a complete waste of time.)

Her blood pressure *was* high, despite the prescription she's been taking. The doctor said the situation called for rest and further observation.

So Iola spent all day Saturday at Sunrise Hospital. She was there Saturday night and Sunday, too, until Sunday afternoon, when Dr. Weinberg came on his rounds to evaluate Iola and determine if she was well enough to be released.

He said, "Well, Ms. Heugely, we've talked about your high blood pressure and your medications. Are you experiencing any stresses in your life?"

Iola said, "Stress? Boy, *I'll* say. It's the Sunbeams. To tell you the truth, they're driving me crazy."

Dr. Weinberg said, "The sun beams?"

Iola said, "Yep. I try to stay in charge, but them Sunbeams won't sit still. They bounce all over the room, and some run out the door and down the hall."

Young Dr. Weinberg started to flip through Iola's chart. "Hmmm," he said. "The sun beams run down the hall, do they? Have you told anybody about this?"

Iola said, "I sure did. I told the president."

"Really!" Dr. Weinberg said.

"You bet," Iola said.

Dr. Weinberg said, "What did the president tell *you*?"

"She said Sunbeams are like that. I'm just going to have to learn to deal with them. And you know, I think now she's right."

Dr. Weinberg said, "Let me make sure I'm not missing anything here, Ms. Heugely. I know some people *are* sensitive to sun beams. Do they cause you a rash or anything?"

"A rash?" Iola said. "Nope."

Dr. Weinberg said, "What is the biggest problem these sun beams are causing?"

"Well, it's the noise," Iola said. "They just won't quit talkin'."

"The noise?" Dr. Weinberg said. "The sun beams are *talking to you?*"

Iola was not sure she liked the tone of his voice. "Well, *yes*," she said. "But mostly, they just talk."

Dr. Weinberg was making notes on her chart as fast as he could. And he wasn't sure this residency in internal medicine had prepared him to handle such a raging psychosis. "I see," he said. "I see. Can anybody *else* hear them talking?"

Iola looked at him like he was a couple of bales short of a full haystack, and then—it *dawned* on her! She said, "You're not a *member,* are you?"

Well, just about then, Brock and Kaelynne came from the church—where they'd been to meetings—and they vouched for Iola, and they vouched for the Sunbeams, and the hospital let her go.

Monday was Memorial Day. They spent it away from the crowds and the noise, just relaxing in the shade up on Mt. Charleston.

They set up the folding chairs. They put a cloth over the picnic table. They put a watermelon in the creek. They brought macaroni salad and Kentucky Fried Chicken with biscuits for lunch. And a tray of marshmallow Rice Krispie treats.

Some of them played Rook. Some of them played Uno. It was a lovely day. It was calm. It was cool. And Iola felt *much* better. And a good time WAS had by all, just like EvaDean wrote it in the weekly. Which was good news. Which is all you *really* needed to know about Iola's trip, I suppose.

I hope I haven't embarrassed Iola. I want you to remember it *was* a good trip, in the end. And that *is* good news. So, don't mention the roller coaster to anybody. Okay? Or the Sunbeams. Because Iola's gonna' give 'em another try. And that's good news, too.

Part of that story's in the hometown weekly, the good news newspaper that helps you remember who you are and where you're from.

CLOBY'S CALL

The hometown weekly just came in the mail. I've been through all the headlines, *twice,* and there's really not much to grab you this week, I have to say. Things have been pretty slow. January can be like that in the news business, especially in a place like Parley Grove. Oh, they've got a few filler articles from the extension service:

WINTER GOOD TIME FOR BOX ELDER BUG CONTROL, EXPERTS SAY

And:

INFORMATION PROVIDED ON FOOD LABELS

Not exactly three-alarm headlines, are they?

Even the ever-popular society column by EvaDean Thiede seems to be dragging this week:

OUT 'N ABOUT
By EvaDean Thiede

Dear Readers, This is your column. If you don't tell me your news, I can't write it. So if you didn't call, don't complain.

I think the holidays have been hard on EvaDean.

It's clear the news is slower than usual, even for Parley Grove, when *The Progress* prints the week's lunch menu for the senior citizens' center on the front page!

It looks like Iola down there's cooking up a storm.

On Monday, she's fixing pigs in a blanket. That's bacon-wrapped hot dogs, stuffed with cheese.

On Tuesday, Italian sausage in gravy.

Wednesday: Ham and funeral potatoes.

Thursday: Southern-fried chicken fingers and tater-tots.

And Friday: Burgers and fries.

As you can see, Iola's gonna *kill* those old people. It won't be intentional. She eats it herself. Even finishes what they don't. The only waste (waist) anything goes to is *Iola's*.

She's a good woman, Iola is—a good woman who's battling a frightful condition. She's locked in a struggle with Thin Iola, who's trapped inside her body and who's trying to get out. Every now and again, Thin Iola wakes up. She roars to life like an evil spirit who is trying to get out, trying to make Real Iola eat stuff like celery and watercress, trying to make her gag when she sees chocolate cream pie, making her think about buying a treadmill. She gives Real Iola ridiculous impulses like that.

It's pretty scary when Thin Iola tries to take control. Real Iola used to be afraid that she would lose this battle of will—that she'd just be vanquished and disappear. But now, after years of experience with Thin Iola, Real Iola's learned that she can knock her out down there pretty easily with three or four Ding Dongs. Or she can dump a plate of nachos and cheese on her. That'll keep her quiet for a while. A few scoops of burnt almond fudge ice cream is another effective remedy. So she's learned to manage her condition, and she'll be all right. I don't think you need to worry.

No, the news is pretty thin in *The Progress* this week. But the ads are there, as always. There's the usual full-page ad on the last page—page six—for LaPriel's Real Deal Mart. Number-two-and-a-half-size canned peaches are on sale for sixty-nine cents for anybody who didn't have the good sense to put up their own last fall.

And just before that is the quarter-page county merchants' directory—that block of little square ads that show up every week:

**Gloyd's   Hardware: Largest
selection. If it's in stock, we have it.**

There are always a few want ads every week that earn *The Progress* a few dollars:

Next to the want ads, you've got the legal notices of the trustee sales and the usual water meetings. Here's one, and it's the strangest legal notice in *The Progress* I've ever seen—a notice, published in the weekly by order of the court, that Cloby Stubsted has changed his name.

The man went out and legally changed his name! The name he's had for sixty-two years, and it wasn't working for him any more! The name, all this time, by which he's been known upon the records of the Church, here upon the earth, and to Social Security and to the IRS and to Publishers Clearing House Sweepstakes, and to *everybody* in Parley Grove—his *own name,* and he's changed it!

When you consider the names you hear in Parley Grove, you could think Cloby got off easy. Coulda done a lot worse! I'd give you examples, but I don't want to offend anybody. And you *know* which names *they* are. But now plain old "Cloby Stubsted"—actually, it's "Clobert"—no longer fits the man. He felt the need for something more—more *substantial.*

That may sound silly to you, but it's understandable if you know what's happened to Cloby. Because a lot has changed lately in his life. A lot. And *that* was first mentioned in the weekly about five or six weeks ago, under the headline:

CHANGES ANNOUNCED BY CHURCH

That's a better headline than it sounds. It was a good headline that really grabbed people. Because the Mormons in Parley Grove kinda like to see Church things changed every now and again. The Lord is the same, yesterday, today, and forever, but the Church moves things around once in a while. And they *like* that change, Mormons do—*especially* the ones in Parley Grove, where it's about the only change they ever get.

Yes, that headline—**Changes Announced by Church**—made 'em read the page twice to make sure they didn't miss any of it. Just *anticipating* Church changes is Parley Grove's favorite indoor sport. And just before a local conference comes around, the anticipation turns to speculation. And things sometimes get out of hand as people start to imagine what or who might get changed, though I doubt anybody guessed Cloby.

A catchy headline like **Changes Announced by Church** is almost tabloid. It can make you wonder. It opens the door *juuuust* enough to get your imagination going. *Changes!* Who knows what that means? Maybe—maybe they'll change it so people who come to meeting early have to sit on the front row instead of the back. That'd be a change!

Or change the meetings so the organist has to follow the conductor instead of the other way around.

Make 'em tell the boys they won't just play basketball next Tuesday night, and have 'em *mean* it, for once! Real *changes!* I don't say that to be sacrilegious. Really, I don't. But you say *change* and *church* in the same headline, and people feel free to imagine the possibilities. Like the Higbee girl: Euzell and Verlene's daughter, Eulene, wishes they'd change the no-hugging rule for missionaries. Just at the airport, of course. She's going up to Salt Lake next week to see Clade Merkeley off for Papua, New Guinea. They say he's going clear over there to preach the word to the children of cannibals. Which means he's a generation too late. I'd say the Merkeley boy and real cannibals is a fair match. I'm just amazed he passed the interview!

But some people—and I mean even the good people in Parley Grove—when they hear there's going to be a change in the Church, they can't help imagining that something might loosen up somewhere, even though they *know,* in their heart of hearts, that change *really* means that somebody's life is about to be fastened down tighter. In the case of Cloby Stubsted, a *lot* tighter. As changes go, this one's pretty big. So big, in fact, everybody in Parley Grove heard about it immediately—even the ones who didn't go to conference heard about Cloby. Even the fifteen Baptists and eleven Catholics in Parley Grove heard about him.

No presiding authority from Salt Lake came down for the conference. Some people thought this might not have happened if one *had*. Not that they think any less of President RDell C. Markum than they do of somebody from Salt Lake. Then, again, nobody from Salt Lake is the county assessor in Parley Grove. But *I* believe that President Markum gave the matter careful thought and deliberation and fervent prayer. And I believe that the call extended to Cloby Stubsted came as inspiration from heaven. You should believe it, too. Because nobody on *earth* would have thought of it!

We shouldn't have been so surprised it was Cloby, though, because there were signs that he was being prepared. You just had to know where to look for them—in places besides in his closet next to the furnace in the basement of the high school.

Truth is, ever since he went up to Provo to have 'em work on his prostate, Cloby has been a different man. That was nearly a year ago. And a man can change a lot in a year.

Cloby still starts his morning with the boys down to the ChatNChew—home of the world-famous ParleyBerry Pie—*if* the school furnace is working. He goes to the school to check it every morning about six. It's an old furnace that was due for replacement eight years ago, but the district is trying to stretch its budget.

When the boiler's temperamental, Cloby fixes it with a technique he's learned through years of trial and error. It's a secret. He won't say much about the way he fixes the boiler. But it involves incremental turns of the isolator valve and the pressure release wheel that have to be timed *down to the second,* followed by resetting the fuse on the blower switch, followed by three good hard whacks on the manifold with the biggest pipe wrench he's got. Then he hits the reset button, and it fires right up. Every time. And it'll work just fine again for another two days or maybe three weeks. But that's Cloby's secret, and it's job security for a janitor. In fact, Cloby's furnace skill has earned him quite a reputation.

As I said, when it's working, he heads over to the ChatNChew, where there's been one sign of his preparation. Athlene says that after nineteen years of waitressing, she's now pouring one fewer cup of coffee every morning and one more cup of hot chocolate. And that's been going on for ten months. And the difference is Cloby!

Cloby's wife, Chlorine, has been out of the habit of fixing him breakfast for at least thirty-five years, since she never would allow coffee in the house. And she sleeps in until nearly 7:00 anyway. So after he stops at the school, Cloby arrives at the ChatNChew by about 6:30—not for coffee any more, and not just for the breakfast, but for the company, mostly; to be with the boys, with Vernus and Buzz and Cleelan and Wink and all of 'em.

They get there early to tackle all the latest topics. They talk about . . . oh, they talk about, uh, elk—that bull that Laron *barely* missed three years ago.

They talk about football—PG's prospects for *next* season, since they didn't do so well this year, and how they went all the way to state in 1961.

They talk some about UN conspiracies. Vernus says he's sure he "seen one of them black helicopters up over Baldy" when he was fishing last summer.

And they talk about the year when the county road crew finally blacktopped the street and then dug it up the very next week to put through a water pipe.

So it's mostly current affairs that they talk about. It's a chance to catch up on the latest. Some days Cloby orders the sausage and eggs, and some days the biscuits and gravy. But he's kicked the coffee habit, after all those years, with no help from the boys. And that's *one* big change in his life: no more coffee. And when they all finish, Cloby gets Athlene to fix him up with a great big Coke—for the road, you know—when he leaves.

He's not addicted to it or anything. But it does make him feel better. Makes him feel brighter. And if it'll do that for Cloby, you can't begrudge him. Besides, it makes his headache go away.

Well, on the Wednesday morning before the conference, Cloby was in there with the boys, just about to leave, when President RDell C. Markum himself came in the door of the ChatNChew. Buzz saw him first, and gave the fellas a sign. It got real quiet there at the counter. President Markum moved toward the empty stool next to 'em all, looking pretty awkward in his blue suit. The boys were looking just as awkward with their hats pulled down low. Finally Wink (who says *he* "don't care") said, "So! RDell. You collectin' taxes or tithing today? We all just give our last dime to Athlene."

President Markum said, "Morning, boys."

A few of 'em mumbled back, "Morning, RDell." "Morning, Pres'dunt."

Just then, Athlene came to the counter carrying Cloby's big Coke, about to say something when *she* saw the president. Thinking the better of it, she said, "Cloby, here's your *root beer.*"

Athlene has learned discretion from nineteen years of waitressing at the ChatNChew in Parley Grove.

Well, turned out, *Cloby* was the man President Markum had come to see. The other boys all scattered pretty quick.

"Brother Stubsted," President RDell C. Markum said, "I need to meet with you in my office."

"Do ya?" Cloby said. "The one to the courthouse, or the one to the church?"

"The one at the church," President Markum said.

Cloby looked thoughtful. "Well, okay. I suppose I'll be there Sunday."

President Markum said, "I was hoping to see you this evening. And I'd like you to bring Chlorine."

Well, at that moment, right there in the ChatNChew, time stood still. Cloby's heart raced, and he felt weak in the knees.

And that's how it happens, isn't it? Just when you're minding your own business—finishing breakfast, or fixing the furnace, or mending your net— you hear the call . . . the call that will change your life. What happened at the ChatNChew, of course, was just the call *to* the call. Cloby didn't know what the actual call would be. But he could see something coming.

Cloby's call, as I said, should not have been so surprising. He's always been a good-hearted man. This winter he has been using the blade on his pickup to clear the widows' driveways. And his language hasn't been nearly as colorful since he sold off the last of his sheep. And, as he's gotten a bit older, he's taken on a sort of sweetness. Sweetness is a blessing that comes to some men, gradually, with age. Sweetness and prostate trouble. I don't want to give the impression that Cloby's over the hill, because he's not. He's just at that stage in a man's life when the healthiest cells in his body are the ones that grow hair in his ears and his nose.

Chlorine told Cloby he couldn't wear his overalls to the interview. She knows the protocol of these things, since she was raised by a Sunday School superintendent. So, even though it was only Wednesday, Cloby put on his best (and only) western suit. Brown double-knit polyester never wears out, though it may not fit the same after thirty years. He put a bolo tie under the collar of his best shirt, the one with the pearlescent snap buttons down the front and over the pockets, and got out the smallest belt buckle he could find. They were both too nervous to eat supper that evening, Cloby and Chlorine were, thinking about what might be coming to them. So they just sat there in the kitchen, all dressed up and pretty quiet, until about a quarter to seven, when Cloby said, "Well, Mother, I guess it's time we'd better go."

In the office at the church, President RDell C. Markum was surrounded by his two counselors, DuWayne D. Dorton and LaMont K. Ovard. It doesn't get more intimidating than that to a member of the flock in Parley Grove. But they told Cloby the Lord loves him. Which, of course, He does. And then they extended the call.

He was speechless. Just speechless. That was not a great sign, considering what he'd just been called to do.

But could he do it? Could he be such, after all the great men he'd known in that calling, men of wisdom and wit, will and wind? Was Cloby cut from that same cloth? He felt so inadequate. That was all right, because it's good to be humble. If you're humble, the Spirit can work with you. But it didn't prompt Cloby with much to say. Finally, Chlorine volunteered that she was just so proud of him. And then Cloby said he would do his best, if they were sure that's what they wanted, and what the *Lord* wanted him to do. Which they *were*. So in no time it was over, and Cloby and Chlorine were out the door, facing the future with fear and trembling.

By the time they got home, Cloby had found not only his voice again, but his resolve. He turned off the truck, turned off the headlights, and clung to the wheel as he said to Chlorine, "Mother, if I'm gonna be this, I'm gonna *be* 'er whole hog. I'm gonna give 'er all I got. I will act and look the part." Which is the right attitude.

Chlorine started to tear up at the thought of what a righteous man he was.

The next day, Thursday, Cloby left the school early to make a run to Richfield with Chlorine before Christensen's Department Store closed. He bought himself a new suit—a blue wool blend—and a white shirt and a city tie. In the book department, he picked out the start of his new gospel library: *Mormon Doctrine; The Work and the Glory,* the nine-volume set on cassette, unabridged; and *Especially for Mormons,* volumes three, four, and five.

But Cloby's luckiest find in there was the new paperback release, *High Council Talks for Dummies.* And the money for all of it came out of what Cloby's been saving for his lifelong dream of owning a Winnebago.

Saturday he went to VarDell's Barber Shop and had VarDell trim up what little hair he has. He shined his best boots, and by Sunday, he was ready to look the part. A hush fell over the conference as his name was read: Clobert Stubsted—a hush, then whispers, followed by a few smiles and shaking heads as the Saints were constrained to acknowledge that God does indeed move in mysterious ways, His wonders to perform. But they all voted for him. Give them credit for that. Unanimous in the affirmative. And true to the faith.

It should have been the proudest day of Cloby's life as he stood and took that long walk up the aisle toward his new seat among the ranks. It was the *longest* walk of his life, and all the while the stiff collar on his new white shirt was threatening to choke him to death. He'd done all a man could do to prepare in four days. And he had repented of his every sin. What more could he ask of himself? But his sense of inadequacy overwhelmed him. Just overwhelmed him. He could feel people staring at the back of his neck; he could tell what the congregation was thinking. He was not *clueless* about this. He could compare himself with the other men on the stand and see what everybody else could see.

The difference was dignity.

You don't get dignity by putting on a blue suit. He knew that *those* men had dignity, and they must have had it all their lives.

Cloby knew he'd *didn't* have it, and he never had.

And now here he came, trembling, in response to the call, walking up the aisle in slow motion, wondering how he could ever rise to the dignity of his new peers. By the time he reached the stand, Cloby was feeling lower than a duck's waddle—a feeling that can put you in the proper position to be inspired.

It was in the depths of his humility that the inspiration came. It came to Cloby as he took his place among the likes of those dignified men of the high council . . .

Trussler M. Perkley
Sardis R. Fackler
Othnol V. Aagard
L. Ercell Salvesen (*that* brother's a pillar!)
Lavenard B. Windborg
Norval J. Mackleprang
LaFaun Q. Bithell
Faddis W. Henroid
Delmo K. Petersen
LaRell J. Odle (who is a dear soul)
and, finally,
O. Bernon Crump

Cloby considered their ways. Then he considered his. And in that *flash* of insight and inspiration he saw just as clear as a hump on a camel the true nature of what it was they had that gave them dignity—what they had that he did not: an initial! Cloby did not have *an initial*.

You parents of children, yet unborn! Remember this lesson: Don't do that to your sons! Don't send them forth into the world with the disability of just a first and last name as if that were enough! It can hold them back all their lives. I give you Cloby as the example, and I rest my case.

But give that man credit for correcting his parents' mistake at his stage of life. For having the insight, the humility, the nerve, and the gumption, at age sixty-two, to go down to the courthouse and fill out the papers and pay the fee and publish the notice in *The Parley's Progress* to have his name made whole: Clobert T. Stubsted. Cloby *T.* The *T* doesn't *stand* for anything, but it *sounds* so good! It is dignified. He tried out all twenty-six letters. *T* is the most dignified one. *Cloby T.*

Doing this thing has made Cloby feel better than he's felt in his whole life. He's complete now. He's fixed, and he's fully ready to serve.

After Cloby spent some time studying the new talk book he bought, he asked President RDell C. Markum when his first talk would be.

President Markum said, "Well, Cloby, giving talks, you know, that's just *one* of the things high councilmen do. And it's not even the most important. I think we have speaking covered for the next little while," he said. "The *important* part of the call is that special portion of the work you oversee. It's what'll take up the most of your time, though most people aren't even aware of it. We've given your assignment careful thought and prayer, Brother Stubsted, and we'd like *you* to be in charge of—it's a big responsibility—to be in charge of facilities. All the church buildings in the Parley Grove Stake. To make sure they're well cared for and in good repair. And I know you are the right man for the job."

At that moment, something whispered in Cloby's heart that he really *was*—his own assurance that he was the man for the job, with the job for the man. And that put him at peace with the world. *And* with heaven.

"And one thing, Cloby, that you'll probably want to look at right away," President Markum said. "We've been having some trouble with a furnace."

Part of that story's in the hometown weekly, the good news newspaper that helps you remember who you are and where you're from.

NEW CAR

The hometown weekly just came in the mail. EvaDean Thiede starts out this week with:

OUT 'N ABOUT
By EvaDean Thiede

A few robins have been seen in Parley Grove this week. Do they know something that we don't? Still no sign of daffodils.

Then she launches into the meaty stuff.

A commendable demonstration on self-defense and crime fighting was presented last week by the Boy Scout troop of the Parley Grove First Ward. Attending were various people who all said the boys did a fine job, and it makes us glad we don't have much call for self-defense around here.

> **Passing a kidney stone last week was Dax Ipson. Marneece says it was the worst one he's ever had, and it laid him up for two days, but he's a much happier camper now.**
>
> **LaEarl and NonaRene Nelford went to Salt Lake last week to visit their son, Vonelle, and came home with a new car. They bought it from LaEarl's cousin's nephew who owns the car lot. NonaRene says they got a real deal. And if you've seen NonaRene out driving this week, you know it's a beauty. Congratulations, NonaRene!**

Well, we should all be happy for NonaRene. It's time she had a new car. At her stage of maturity, she shouldn't have to be driving a pickup any more. She's been telling LaEarl for a long time she wanted a *sedan*. No sense having two trucks at their age. LaEarl's old truck was enough to keep—and it was the one to keep, since it *is* the one that fits the camper for the elk hunt. (And NonaRene always does get her elk.) So NonaRene told him—for about the thirty-sixth time—she was due to have a nice car, a grandma kind of a car, something that would let her drive more than two other ladies to the DUP meeting. And some of those ladies are now getting to where it's hard for them to climb up into the cab of a truck, and she said, "I just believe we ought to be thinking about *them*." That's what she said to LaEarl two weeks ago Monday morning as she was slicing his hash browns and turning his bacon.

LaEarl was staring out the window from the kitchen table, and only half heard what she said. He already knew he was going to give on this one. He was just thinking how *far* he'd have to give. LaEarl is a good husband. And with forty-eight years of marriage now, he's learned to pay attention to his wife. So he said she could have a car. It'd be for their anniversary. Because LaEarl *is* a romantic at heart, he would go against his better judgment *just this one time*. But he wasn't *keen* on getting anything too fancy-schmancy so late in the game. And just on principle, it did seem somehow wasteful to LaEarl to get rid of the Silverado, when it was still running perfectly well. It doesn't burn *that* much oil. And he put new tires on her, what, just three years ago. *Still* good tread left. And that battery owes him at least another two years.

To abandon a perfectly good 1988 Silverado just because she's got a few miles on her and her tailgate is rusted out goes against the grain of this man. He is from Parley Grove, and he is from true pioneer stock. He has lived by the motto, which you younger people should learn: *"Use it up, wear it out, make it do, or do without."* That's just part of who LaEarl *is*. It was bred into him—into him and most everybody he knows. Parley Grove, after all, is not still hanging on because people there have been big spenders. I'll say *not!* Frugality, my friends, is bred into all of us with roots in Parley Grove. It was just bred a little truer in LaEarl.

LaEarl is the man you read about a few years ago in the city papers who got his finger stuck in the coin return of a pay phone in Salt Lake City when it didn't give his quarter back. The paramedics came and tried to get his finger out. They couldn't do it. The fire department came and tried to get his finger out. They couldn't do it. So they brought in a cutting torch and cut the phone off of its base, and they took LaEarl and his finger and the phone to the University Hospital, where they worked on him for a couple of hours before they finally got that finger out in one piece. And when they got it out and bandaged it up, LaEarl said, "Where'd you put my quarter?"

NonaRene turned the eggs over easy and stuck *her* finger in the pan of milk to see if it was hot enough for the cocoa.

NonaRene is a frugal woman. I don't want to give you the wrong impression. She could not have raised the kids on LaEarl's pay from the county road crew if she had been some kind of a spendthrift. But these are supposed to be their golden years, she figured, and NonaRene has always wanted a sedan—something they could take nice vacations in—not a station wagon and not a truck, which is all she's had to drive for forty-eight years.

LaEarl looked up at the wall calendar from the IFA. It was still on February with the picture of Bryce Canyon in the snow. And here it was, *March* already. He got up and turned the page to the new month with a scene of Monument Valley, and right away LaEarl started missing Bryce Canyon. February's was a good picture, he thought. And February was so short. Seemed a waste to be done with that picture so soon.

LaEarl is a man who would be wearing the same socks he wore the day he got married if NonaRene hadn't thrown them away. When he found out last Christmas that she paid $29 for his new flannel shirt, it nearly killed 'im. He *loves* that shirt. But for LaEarl, spending money on *anything* is sooo hard.

As he sat down and braced himself for what he was about to say, he said, "Well, I suppose when we go up to Salt Lake this week we could take a look at what they got on the lot." Just the sound of his words made him start to feel faint.

Both LaEarl and NonaRene understood that the lot they would check with would be the one owned by LaEarl's mother's brother's daughter's husband's sister's boy, Mahonri. He sells used cars in West Valley City. That way they would not only keep business in the family, almost, but they would keep themselves from getting taken by some big-city fast-talkers who might treat them like hicks.

People from Parley Grove do not like to be taken, and they do not like people who are condescending, either. And it can be intimidating for people like the Nelfords to do business in a strange place with people they don't know. And up in Salt Lake these days it's even hard to tell any more whether you're dealing with Church people or not. So they were glad to have Mahonri Lemon on a good recommendation. And before they left Parley Grove they called ahead, long distance, to make sure he would be there.

NonaRene set the plates on the table. She got out the butter and her homemade peach jelly.

She said, "I seen a beauty of a car up to Richfield last week. It was big. And sort of gold. I think it was a Buick or something like that."

"Holy Hannah!" LaEarl said. "Don't be lookin' at Buicks. We'll get you a car, but we ain't gonna be puttin' on airs."

NonaRene took the ketchup out of the fridge and put it on the table.

LaEarl looked up at her and said, "You don't want automatic transmission, do you, Mother?"

She said, "I sure do."

LaEarl winced. "Well," he said, "the hard thing about automatics is that they make it rough to ever go back to a stick. 'Sos I hear."

NonaRene said, "I don't plan on *goin'* back, Earl. I'm sixty-nine years old, and I should drive an automatic!"

She set the plate of toast down in front of him with an extra thud.

"Well, all right, Mother," he said. "I guess you can have an automatic, seein's how here we don't need air conditioning."

NonaRene narrowed her eyes. "Automatic AND air conditioning!"

LaEarl said, "But we wouldn't use the air conditioning from—from September 'til June. That'd be such a waste."

NonaRene said, "I might just want to use the air conditioning in *January!* Open the windows and turn 'er up full blast if I get a mind to."

She smiled at him. She winked at him. She was *playing* with him. This was a dance they had danced before. They have danced this dance on every purchase they've ever made.

There was a long silence. Then LaEarl said, "Okay, Rene, for *you*—nuthin' but the best. Now sit down, and I'll bless the food."

So on Thursday, LaEarl gassed up the Silverado for its farewell trip to Salt Lake. He took out the gun rack, because on a trade-in he'd never get out of it what he originally paid. But with no gun rack they felt sort of vulnerable heading up there to the city. So NonaRene went to the closet and got out a .22 pistol that she put in her purse, along with her concealed weapon permit, and the Happenings discount book for Salt Lake she'd bought from her grandson.

NonaRene had packed their lunch: egg salad sandwiches, and carrot sticks, and celery strips, and oatmeal cookies, and apples, and two cans of Shasta root beer.

They had good weather all the way up to Salt Lake. And LaEarl was talkative, much more than usual, which was *fine*. But he talked mostly about how well the old Silverado was running, how she still had lots of pep in her. How the radios on these older trucks are so much better than the ones in the new ones. How she wasn't due for an oil change for another 800 miles. How cars nowadays are so computerized you can't hardly work on 'em yourself any more. How car dealers charge you all those document fees that are just another way for 'em to stick ya'.

LaEarl just couldn't help himself. He didn't mean to spoil the fun. He didn't. He really didn't. He was even planning on taking NonaRene out to lunch while they were in Salt Lake to celebrate their anniversary, their forty-eighth anniversary. There's a wonderful restaurant up there LaEarl just loves. Nothing like it in Parley Grove. It's so much fancier than the ChatNChew. And it has the *best* food, just like home-cooked. And nice atmosphere. You can have anything you want. And it is because LaEarl *is* a romantic at heart he planned to take NonaRene for their forty-eighth anniversary to Chuck-O-Rama. And because they don't use waiters, you don't have to tip 'em, and you don't feel bad about it, either.

No, LaEarl was *not* trying to spoil the drive. It's just *sooo* hard for him to give up on something that's not certifiably shot. That's just who he is. Not stingy. Just tight. Tighter than that truck's rusted lug nuts.

But his monologue didn't bother NonaRene. She'd heard it all before. She simply tuned it out just like she did the road noise coming up through the hole in the floorboard. NonaRene was thinking about bucket seats and an automatic transmission, and maybe even a cup holder.

They got to Vonelle and Kamae's place in West Valley in good time, before Vonelle or the kids were home from school. (Vonelle teaches shop.)

So they left their suitcase with Kamae and drove over to Mahonri Lemon's
car lot, which was not too far away. It's a small lot on 3500 South in West
Valley City, under a sign that says *Latter-day Cars and Vinyl Siding*—a good
name for Mahonri's business. At first he called it *Lemon Auto,* but he nearly
went broke.

Mahonri had LaEarl and NonaRene come in and sit down across from
his desk. He gave them some popcorn. He said how he'd seen in the *Church
News* a few weeks ago that his uncle (and LaEarl's cousin), Sherald Turpin,
was going to be a mission president. And LaEarl said, "Yep, I seen it, too."
LaEarl was relieved; it was a sign he was dealing with an honest salesman.

Mahonri said, "Well, what can I do for you good people today?"

NonaRene opened her mouth like she was going to say something, and
LaEarl pushed his knee into her thigh. LaEarl said, "Well, my wife's been
thinking—I mean, *we* have—that pretty soon, or maybe one of these days
here, she might want to be drivin' another car. And sos if you was to have the
right sort of thing at the right sort of price—*if you know what I mean*—and
if you was to make us a real good offer on that nice Silverado out there, and
if all together it was a *rill dill* 'n all, well, we might be willin' to just have a
look around."

Mahonri said, "Wonderful. That's great. Tell me about the sort of car
you're thinking of."

NonaRene opened her mouth again. And LaEarl kneed her again. But
this time, she kneed him back! She said, "Well, I don't want one of them cars
from Japan or one of them foreign places over there, 'cause you know what
they're like. But I want something with automatic and air conditioning. And
cup holders! And my favorite color is gold."

Mahonri said, "Perfect."

Three hours later, they drove off the lot in a blue 2004 Ford Taurus LX.
It was a magnificent car! Blue is NonaRene's second-favorite color. And it's
a nice blue. And LaEarl could still hold *his* head high, because the 2004
Taurus was still under warranty—sort of—and Mahonri gave him a *real*
deal, and he figured a car like this could last them the rest of their lives. And
NonaRene got everything she'd ever dreamed of. It was a beautiful blue, and
it had automatic transmission, and air conditioning, and cup holders. And an
AM-FM radio. And floor mats!

Well they drove this gorgeous new car (with air conditioning and cup
holders) over to show it off to Vonelle's family. Oh, they were impressed!
Everybody was so impressed. Then Vonelle announced he had tickets that
night for himself and the boys and for LaEarl—three generations of the

Nelfords, fathers and sons—to the Monster Truck Challenge at the E Center, with the defending champion, Dieselsaurus, with one thousand horsepower and *seven* thousand pounds of steel. Wasn't that wonderful? And LaEarl had never seen a Monster Truck Challenge before. So this night was going to be a real party: boys to the truck challenge, girls to the mall. Boys in Vonelle's minivan, and girls in the new Taurus. "If you *want*," LaEarl said.

Well, NonaRene *had* looked forward to going to the Valley Fair Mall. There are no really fancy stores like that in Parley Grove—no Mervyn's or Penney's or ZC—whatever they call ZCMI these days. And NonaRene was thinking about a new housedress, and maybe some slippers. But then the baby threw up, and Kamae said she had better stay home and that NonaRene had better go to the mall by herself.

NonaRene lost a little of her nerve. She had never been to a mall in the city by herself. She always had somebody with her before. And the Valley Fair Mall is such a huge place.

Kamae said, "Don't worry, Mom. I'll be fine. And you'll be fine. Really. I know you planned to shop."

NonaRene was feeling tolerably timid as she got behind the wheel of that amazing new car—that 2004 Ford Taurus LX LaEarl had entrusted to her—to drive it the two miles to the Valley Fair Mall. The traffic on 3500 South was terrible. And the automatic transmission threw NonaRene every time she came to a red light, because she wanted to put in the clutch. She just didn't know what to *do* with her left foot. She was feeling pretty nervous about this whole excursion. But she made it to the mall, the Valley Fair Mall, and parked at the far end of the lot. She hoped that out there the sides of that fabulous new car wouldn't be scraped by careless people getting out of their *old* cars. NonaRene was careful to lock it. Checked all four doors. And she went into the mall and found Mervyn's. Oh, such an incredible store!

NonaRene stayed in the mall longer than she planned, and by the time she got outside, it was dark. And not being able to see the mountains, she was disoriented—not sure of her direction as she stepped out to that vast parking lot to find the new car LaEarl had just bought for her, against his better judgment, and entrusted to her care. She clutched her bags and held her purse a little tighter. Being alone in the city is not like being alone in Parley Grove. NonaRene knew *that*. In the city you don't know who people are. You don't know where they're from. You don't know what they're like. You don't know what they might do. She knew this was a time to be wary.

And then, in the dim light of the parking lot, she *saw* it: four men in the act of entering the blue Ford Taurus. Four young men. Four strong men. Four men in the dark, at the edge of the lot, just getting into a 2004 blue

Ford Taurus XL. Later that night, when it was over and she told it all to LaEarl, she said, "Oh, Daddy, I've never been so scared in all my life. They looked to me like they might have been from Iraq or Mexico or from one of them places over *there*."

But in the dim light of the parking lot of the Valley Fair Mall, NonaRene pulled herself together. She said to herself, "Don't panic, Rene." And her fear gave way to rage. She dropped her bags and opened her purse and pulled out the .22 pistol. And she aimed it straight ahead with both arms at the men in the car. And NonaRene Nelford shouted at the top of her lungs, "I got a *gun*, and I know how to use it! You git out of that car right *now!*"

Well, NonaRene was in a good negotiating position. She did not have to ask twice. Four strong, frightened young men jumped out of the blue Ford Taurus and ran.

The heart of a sixty-nine-year-old woman is not supposed to beat as fast as NonaRene's did. But when her knees stopped shaking and when the men were gone, she picked up her bags and put them in the back seat, got in behind the wheel, and locked the doors.

Her hands were still shaking when she opened her purse *again* and felt for the keys. She was shaking so bad she couldn't get the key into the ignition. She tried it again. She tried yet again, and still it wouldn't go in. She turned it over the other way, and it still wouldn't go in.

Then NonaRene looked out the window, and what she saw brought back all the panic. A different panic. A *worse* panic. A panic that overwhelmed her, as it all became clear—because there, one row ahead, and about six stalls to the left, she saw a blue 2004 Ford Taurus LX with a temporary license plate.

After all that, my friends, what would *you* have done?

I am pleased to tell you that NonaRene Nelford is an honest woman. She believes in both rights *and* responsibility. So she unloaded her stuff and put it in the right car. And on the back of her Mervyns receipt, she wrote with a pencil "Sorry," and she put it under the windshield wiper of the *other* blue Ford Taurus. And then, to her credit, this woman drove across the street to the police station at the West Valley City Hall to confess her story.

She barely started in to it when the officer pointed to the other end of the counter and said, "You mean *them?*"

NonaRene turned and saw four men—four strong young men, four ashen-looking men—reporting a carjacking by a little old lady, just over five feet tall, with gray hair and glasses and a mean-looking gun.

The *good* news is, no shots were fired, nobody got hurt, no charges were filed, thank goodness—and, *thank goodness again*—none of it got on television. That's news *so* wonderful, it was just *too special* for NonaRene to tell EvaDean and have her put that whole part in the weekly. Not secret. Just very special and personal and private. So don't trifle with it. Okay?

But *part* of it was *there,* the *good* news part about NonaRene in the newest car in Parley Grove—*good* news for a change—in the hometown weekly, the *good* news newspaper that helps you remember who you are and where you're from.

THE
PARLEY'S PROGRESS

SERVING PARLEY GROVE, UTAH'S 87TH LARGEST CITY, AND ALL OF TAYLOR COUNTY

MOTHER'S DAY

The hometown weekly just came in the mail. EvaDean Thiede starts out this week with:

OUT 'N ABOUT
By EvaDean Thiede

CORRECTION: Due to a typographical error that was not my fault, this column last week said Arlafaye Hooley went up to Salt Lake for a fancy dinner and died at Market Street Grill. Oops! Of course, she just di*n*ed there. Sorry we were wrong, Arlafaye. [Which, once again, is not exactly what EvaDean meant to say.]

Then she writes:

After a week of nice weather, a few optimists are already planting zucchini. The rest of us are keeping our snow boots handy, just in case.

Then EvaDean moves on to one of her meatiest reports of the year:

> **Our little town swelled in numbers last weekend with all the visitors for Mother's Day. Among the many returning home to our beautiful valley for the occasion were . . .**

. . . and then EvaDean devotes nineteen column inches to their names— the names of the expatriates and their children . . . those displaced persons who returned as refugees from the world they once set out to conquer . . . that vast Parley Grove diaspora who gathered home, because the tie still binds, and not just to their mother, but to this *place*. They come back, because they haven't forgotten their roots. They come back, because where else would they want to be other than this wonderful place—their home town? These are the names—nineteen column inches of names—of people who remembered not just their mother, but remembered who they are.

And if your mother or grandmother lives in Parley Grove and your name is not on that list, *your* name, my friend, is mud! You are some mother's heartache. You are some family's sorrow. They don't put very many demands on you if you've left and gone away. Just Thanksgiving and Christmas and Mother's Day. That is all they ask.

Versal Euler was fixing up around his place the week before Mother's Day, expecting some of the Eulers might come home. There are five of them, Versal and Vertis's kids, all moved away now; four of them, at least, pretty permanently. The youngest is still out there trying to find herself somewhere, and making quite a game of it. It's a game of hide-and-seek for Destry, and she plays both offense and defense at the same time.

Versal got to straightening the woodpile out to the side of the house. Found a rat's nest in there, so he made a mental note to stop at the feed store to pick up some bait. Versal took down the storm windows and put up the screens, and then spent a good part of the afternoon tinkering with the lawn mower. He'd forgotten to drain the gas last fall, and it had gummed up the works.

Inside, Vertis was making casserole trays of funeral potatoes to put in the freezer so they'd be all ready on Mother's Day. She would be able to thaw out one or two or even three of them, depending on how many Eulers finally came, and she hadn't heard from Destry. In fact, hadn't heard from Destry since February.

The girl's been up in Salt Lake for nearly two years now, ever since she got out of high school, living in a cheap apartment near Liberty Park. She's had different roommates. We don't know where *they* are from, but they're not from around Parley Grove.

In the last year, year and a half, Destry has taken to wearing a lot of black. She *sees* brighter clothes at her job in the pressing room at Salt City Cleaners, but she's *wearing* only black. And now her hair is black, too. And her nails are black. And her skin is pale. She's indoors all day. And she's out late most nights playing electric crash cymbal in a band called Rigor Mortis.

Vertis is worried that Destry might not be going to church up there. And, technically, she's not. But for the last month or so, every Sunday afternoon, Destry has been attending the drum circle in Liberty Park.

Destry doesn't exactly fit in with those people—she doesn't look much like they do, the way she's started dressing only in black—but they accept anybody at the drum circle.

The drum circle, they say, is where people explore their deep relationship with the rhythmical universe and the healing power of the drum in the circle. The drum creates a subsonic vibration, giving a rhythmical massage to everybody near it—affecting each person differently, in his or her own unique and very personal way.

A woman who calls herself "Akeena"—the drum circle facilitator and aura-therapist—says this drum circle massage influences the harmonious alignment of our physical cells and our emotional states and our auras. The drumbeat, she says, echoes the heartbeat, connecting us to our deeper selves.

The drum circle massage makes some people clap, and it makes some people dance, and it makes some people leap on their bare feet and twirl in their tie-dyed skirts. Some people blow smoke rings after a long, slow drag on something that *really* seems to connect them to the cosmos. But they say it's good Karma, the drum circle.

And Destry likes to go. It sort of makes sense to her, that alignment stuff. Which doesn't mean she has thrown out her basic beliefs. No. This is a child who was trained up in the way she should go. In fact, she still wears the CTR ring Vertis gave her when she was nine. But now, she wears it safety-pinned to her left eyebrow.

Akeena—the drum circle facilitator and aura-therapist—says drumming increases our alpha brain waves. Those are the brain waves that relax the tense and energize the tired and heal the emotionally wounded. And that is Destry: emotionally wounded.

Destry and her first roommate were lonely, so they pooled their change and went to a pet store and bought a pet—the best pet they could afford. They bought a pet rat. Named him Mickey. And he's been a good rat. With Mickey, Destry was never alone. Her first roommate left, and others have come and gone since, so Mickey has been Destry's best friend and Destry has been Mickey's best friend.

But back in early March, Mickey developed a hairless lump on his back, and Destry took him to the veterinarian. The vet said he could operate on Mickey. And if he didn't operate, Mickey would die. But he could operate. However, the x-rays and the surgery and the pathology lab and the anesthesia and the post-op recovery nurse and the physical therapy would cost about $600. Destry makes $7.50 an hour. She can barely pay the insurance on her old Plymouth Colt. That was $600 to save a two-year-old-rat, when rats have a life expectancy of two and a half years. But what could she *do?* A friend is a *friend.* And if God sees the sparrow that falls from the sky, then surely He sees the rat with a tumor. So how do you *Choose the Right* for that?

The Mother's Day program in the Parley Grove First Ward would, of course, feature the children—all the kids in Primary, and even the grandkids from out of town. They parade them up to the front of the chapel and put them up there on the stand. The older ones hide in the back and try not to be seen, and the younger ones—especially the Sunbeams—stand in the front and lean out over the rail, and see right there looking back at 'em the biggest audience they've ever had. They see their big chance to *perform!* So they turn their eyelids inside out, and they wave their tongues, and they wave at their mothers, and point and roll their eyes back and giggle. And their mothers look away. The kids try for a while to remember the words to the song that nice lady is working so earnestly to coax out of them: *I know a name, a glorious name, dearer than any other.* They work at it for a while, and then some of 'em give up and pop their eyelids again. And some of 'em pick their noses until they find what they went looking for. They are always the highlight of the Mother's Day service, even though every year at least one mother goes home mortified, in tears at the thought that her offspring would act that way in public, in *church* no less, after all the work she put into getting that kid shined up.

The rest of the mothers have their own issues with the Mother's Day service. Defra Thaxton, the bishop's wife, threatened she wasn't even going to *go* to church this Mother's Day if Varlo Belcher was going to stand up there again and give another sappy tribute to her, the *Mother of the Ward*. Defra said, "I am not their mother! I'm just their phone message service. If they have to have a mother of the ward, let it be Ralphene." Ralphene is president of the Relief Society.

Well, Bishop Thaxton—Bishop Leland D. Thaxton—assured Defra that Varlo would not be speaking at the Mother's Day service this year. Actually, it could be worse. Varlo was going to *sing*. He would once again give his best to his signature number, "That Wonderful Mother of Mine." And when Varlo gets to *"You'll hold a spot down deep in my heart, 'Til the stars no longer shine,"* he always tears up and gets extra vibrato in his throat.

So Varlo would *sing*, and the Mother's Day *talk* this year would fall to Brother Rasmussen, who would say—as that great patriot Abraham Lincoln said—that all that he is, or ever hopes to be, he owes to his angel mother. Brother Rasmussen's angel mother who never spoke a cross word, as he remembers, who toiled from sunup to long past sundown, cheerfully, baking and cleaning and washing and sewing and teaching and loving her twelve grateful children, tucking them in each night with a story and a kiss, after kneeling with each at his or her bedside, before she would freshen up to tend to father's needs.

Ralphene Hedberg threatened last year that if she had to sit through that drippy, sentimental, insipid Mother's Day talk one more time she was gonna stand up in the middle of the service and *scream!*

It's a challenging experience, the annual Mother's Day service. We don't know how it became mandatory. Mother's Day is not mentioned in scripture. Mother's Day did not come across the plains. It's not even in the *Handbook of Instructions*. But it is mandatory. We know that. And every year in the Parley Grove First Ward they put on the Mother's Day service, faithfully. And mothers are still putting up with it as a trial of their faith, because—I guess—that's the kind of creatures mothers are. And because mothers are *energized* by guilt.

At the end of the talk—and it *is* the same talk every year—just when the mothers are ready to confess that they don't measure up, that they are not like the mother in the talk, that they get tired and even cross, and that they sometimes want to say *"You can take this job and shove it!"* we give 'em all a consolation prize. As they go out the door to climb back on their pedestals of guilt, we give 'em a geranium in a plastic pot to take home as a token of our expectations—and as a reminder to try to do better *next* year, and to turn down the pot roast as soon as they get in the door.

Vertis planned to serve pot roast on Mother's Day. It is, after all, Sunday dinner. And even though pot roast usually calls for mashed potatoes, with the projected count now up to twenty-seven, funeral potatoes made in advance was a more practical choice with everything extra Vertis would have to do right after church to put on that spread called Mother's Day dinner—a mother's annual test to see how good a mother she really is.

Of course, some of Vertis's grandkids would make her a card, and the children might remember her with a few thoughtful, practical gifts. But all Vertis *really* wants for Mother's Day is to be together with her family. The *whole* family. No empty chairs. And Destry hadn't returned her phone calls.

Destry's had a lot to deal with all alone up in the city. Mickey Rat made it through the surgery, but he never again had that gleam in his eye, that spring in his step, that twitch in his nose that said, "Hi, glad to see ya." He ate less and less and hardly ever ran in his wheel. Mickey Rat just seemed to be fading away. A week ago Friday, Destry took him back to the animal hospital and checked him in for observation. Saturday she got the urgent message at work: "You'd better come now."

She left right in the middle of pressing a burgundy two-pant suit. Just told her boss she had to go. The Plymouth Colt sputtered as fast as it could go for the seventeen blocks to the animal hospital.

A receptionist ushered Destry into a room called the the grief center. Soft music played on a set of stereo speakers; soft light bathed soft couches; the soft pastel wallpaper had paintings of cherub dogs and cherub cats with halos and wings playing harps in the clouds.

Dr. Bob came in. He said, "I'm so sorry. I did everything I could. You probably want some time with him, alone."

An attendant wheeled in the cart. On the cart was a little pillow. On the pillow, under a tiny sheet, was Mickey. The attendant turned down the sheet to reveal Mickey lying on his back, his four feet up the air, and he left Destry and Mickey to be alone. So hard! And the worst of it: Mickey did not look peaceful. They hadn't even closed his eyes!

After a while, there was a knock on the door, and a man came in the room. He was wearing a lime green blazer with a pastel tangerine tie. He said he was Carston, the grief counselor.

Carston sat down by Destry and opened a thickly padded white book.

Carston said, "These here's your casket options. In that guy's size they run from these real el-cheepo jobs made out of styrene, at $109.99, up through the *good* stuff—for pets that people *really* loved and cared about—with this top-of-the-line number. It's handmade double-walled solid oak with velour lining, and down pillow with needlepoint appliqué. Complete with custom-cast concrete vault, it's $1,300. But because your rat there's been a patient, I can give you $50 off."

Destry sniffed and wiped her eyes with the back of her black sleeve. Carston handed her the box of Kleenex. He said, "We have special arrangements with three cemeteries that will discount the burial plot."

Destry started to cry. She said, "I don't have any money!"

Carston said, "Okay, look, we do cremation for fifty bucks. And the cheapest urn is thirty-five."

Well, Destry doesn't believe in cremation. And Mickey really didn't look good. In fact, he looked pretty much like a dead rat. Destry could tell his spirit was gone.

"So, which one will it be?" Carston said. "I know it's hard, but ya' gotta make up your mind. *Private* pet disposal, you know, is against the law everywhere in the city."

Destry looked up at that man, and she looked around the room, and she saw the place for what it was. She saw her whole world for what it was—which was no place to leave a good and wonderful and treasured friend. She grabbed a handful of Kleenexes out of the box, wrapped them around Mickey, picked him up in her hand, and ran with him out the door, leaving Carston in the grief center to grieve by himself.

And that night, Saturday night, Destry called her mother.

Sunday was a beautiful morning in Parley Grove. Sunshine. The leaves were coming on. A few tulips were still in bloom. The-out-of-towners made for an overflow congregation pulling up to the old brick church. People stood out in the sun, shaking hands and giving hugs, and sharing *How've ya' been?* and *Sure has been a while*. A flock of pigeons spun circles over the steeple in the cloudless blue sky.

In Destry's Plymouth Colt, Parley Grove was more than a five-hour drive. The way that car was running she wondered if she would make it there at all, let alone in time for dinner. She reached the turnoff from Highway 89 on just three cylinders—three cylinders and Vertis's prayers. And now she was back on the familiar road, leading to home, to where everybody would be. She rounded the turn a mile west of town through the alfalfa fields with their sweet purple-blue blossoms, on to where the road runs along the irrigation canal against the poplar trees. She drove past the old county fair barn and the IFA feed store and on 'til the road becomes Main Street—where, on Sunday morning, Mother's Day, everything was closed. The ChatNChew Cafe, LaPriel's Real Deal Mart, and the Taste-E-Freeze were all closed. So, of course, was Clester Holdaway's Parley Rest Motel, which won't open its eight rooms and one family kitchenette (with *some* utensils included) until Memorial Day weekend.

Destry turned right at the stop sign, drove past the brick church on the left surrounded by all of those out-of-town cars, and drove two more short blocks to home—*home,* where Versal had mowed the grass and taken down the storm windows and straightened up the woodpile.

Destry pulled around back and got out of the car. She didn't go inside. She had a mission to fulfill—a last service to a friend. She opened the door to the shed and found a shovel. From the back seat of the car she took a brown paper sack, and she carried the sack and the shovel to find the right spot. She walked all around the yard. She saw a clump of iris poking up through the Johnson grass next to the woodpile. That was a nice spot, there between the woodpile and the flowers. Destry dug the hole. It didn't have to be big. Then out of the sack she took a pencil box—a sturdy cardboard pencil box like we used to get for school. It would fit in the hole pretty well. She eased the box into the hole. She felt like she was done with crying.

Just as she was about to fill in the hole, she noticed that the lid of the box didn't close tight. The little latch was sprung. Destry considered that for a minute, and then she knew just what to do. She unhooked the safety pin from her eyebrow. She pressed it—on an angle—through the side and the top of the box, very carefully, in place of a latch, and fastened it. *Tight.*

She filled up the hole, and patted the dirt down and smoothed it over. And it looked nice, there next to the flowers. It looked peaceful. The whole yard looked good to her. The old house looked better than she remembered when she left it, when all she could think about was getting away.

Destry stood up with the shovel. It had been a long time since she'd worked out in the sun. It felt warm on her shoulders. It felt good on her face. She looked up and saw those pigeons circling overhead. Heard the rustling of their wings. Heard a sound from open windows, two blocks away, the sound of children practicing a song. It was the first human sound she'd heard all day.

Destry hadn't seen a single soul in Parley Grove. That was kind of creepy. And she felt like she wanted to *see* people; she wanted to not be alone any more. So Destry drifted in the direction of the music and, hardly thinking, opened the door of the church. She slipped into the back of the chapel, just as that flock of birds spiraled down and landed on the roof.

The Mother's Day part of the service was just getting underway, with the children filing up to the stand. The little ones popped their eyelids and they picked their noses and they sang, *"Mother so tender and kind and true. . . ."* Varlo Belcher sang, *"You are a wonderful mother, Dear old mother of mine."*

And Brother Rasmussen bore a tearful eulogy to his angel mother, who God made because *He* couldn't be everywhere.

There was, as always, guilt enough to spare.

And they ran out of geraniums in plastic pots.

And the inside of the church bulletin was printed upside down.

And at the organ, Gladys Fackler kept forgetting the fifth flat in the closing hymn.

And yet, it was the *sweetest* service. Destry knew it was. After all the years of doing the same thing, everybody knew it was a beautiful service—in spite of its flaws, in spite of themselves. I'm afraid I don't quite know how to explain it to you. I don't think I *can*. And Destry probably can't, either.

But somehow—somehow—this Mother's Day service brought a little bit of heaven's grace down on Parley Grove. And why shouldn't it have? There are, after all, nineteen column inches here in the weekly of names of the people who came home and were there, and who can tell you I'm speaking the truth.

And in his benediction, LaEarl Nelford fervently prayed that those who did not come this time would be blessed to be able to come next time. And we hope they will. But Destry Euler is one who came.

Vertis got homemade cards from some of the grandchildren. And from her kids, she got the thoughtful, practical gift of more canning jars. And the Eulers finished all three trays of funeral potatoes. The *whole* family was there! And it was the *best* Mother's Day Vertis has ever had. That's good news!

Part of that story's in the hometown weekly, the good news newspaper that will help you remember who you are and where you're from.

THE
PARLEY'S PROGRESS

SERVING PARLEY GROVE, UTAH'S 87TH LARGEST CITY, AND ALL OF TAYLOR COUNTY

BEAUTIFUL WOMEN

The hometown weekly just came in the mail. The big headline this week:

MEETING HELD BY PG CITY COUNCIL

This, of course, happens every month. At least, it's supposed to. And *if* the weekly gets a copy of the council minutes, then sooner or later they get printed in *The Progress*. In fact, they always get printed on the front page, even if there's no real news in them.

It appears the major item of business at the last council meeting was the resolution to commend the volunteer committee who put on this year's Parleybration Dayz. By unanimous vote, it was the best Parleybration ever.

On page two this week, EvaDean Thiede begins with her typical literary introduction:

OUT 'N ABOUT
By EvaDean Thiede

The bigtooth maple are crimson,
the cottonwoods are bronze, and the
quakies are gold. Only fruit left to put
up now are the apples.

Then it says:

> My apologies. The following
> item was inadvertently left out of this
> column a few weeks ago: Recently,
> Shelmer and Arlafaye Hooley visited
> their daughter Sharla Quarenberg and
> her husband J'Wayne in Scipio for the
> blessing of their new baby daughter.
> She was given the name *Hailey Alexis.*

Recently!? It was more than a *month* ago! And EvaDean calls it *recently.* But, she's got to please the Hooleys. And the news doesn't cycle as fast for *The Parley's Progress* as it does for CNN. And it *was* **good** news, and it deserves to be in print in the weekly, and on the record. They can clip this out and paste it in Hailey's scrapbook, and she can keep it all her life. And we hope it's a long and happy life.

Also on page two this week is an obituary and the announcement of a wedding—they were a funeral and a wedding that came much too close together for Ralphene Hedberg. Ralphene is president of the Relief Society in Parley Grove—president of the good Mormon women of the Parley Grove First Ward. And being president of the Relief Society puts her smack dab in the middle of everybody's needs and every woman's problems. *Women's* problems. Men have problems, I suppose, but they don't *talk* about 'em. Reporting problems is the women's job. At least *half* of their problems *are* the men, anyway!

Some days Ralphene's phone just about rings off the hook with all the calls she gets from women who have some sort of need. *Not* that they are dependent on *her.* No. These are women who are self-reliant. They say they will manage, they say they'll be fine, they say they'll get by, but—they just wanted Ralphene to *know,* just thought she ought to be aware, just wanted her to be in the loop. You see, sometimes giving the Relief Society president guilt works faster than simply giving her a request. And people quickly learn how to use the system.

Ralphene's husband, Kanyon, has been reasonably supportive of all this—considering he's a guy and he's put up with it for *three years.* But it's starting to wear on him. Last month, he said he was going to buy Ralphene an answering machine, one that would force people to just cut to the chase.

Kanyon was gonna have it say: "Hello, you've reached the home of the Relief Society president. If you need a visit, press 1. If you want a casserole, press 2. For a babysitter, press 3. To report your visiting teaching, press 4. To report gossiping or backbiting, press 5. To gossip or backbite just a little bit yourself, press 6."

It could come in handy some days. But Ralphene is a compassionate woman—full of good works, full of charity that never fails. But last week charity came close to failing with the funeral and the wedding right on top of each other, and with all there was to do. The scheduling was not just an inconvenience, it was not just a lot of work, it was *traumatic* for Ralphene, because the wedding was Charnelle's, Ralphene's oldest daughter—which, by itself, was good news.

The funeral was Svena Oleson's.

The obituary reads:

> **Svena Oleson died of causes incident to age on Monday, October 12. Born June 16, 1918, in Parley Grove, Utah, to Lars M. and Axelina Bergson Oleson, their only daughter and twelfth child.**
>
> **Attended Parley Grove Grammar School, where she was elected secretary of the fifth-grade class, and Parley Grove High School, where she graduated as valedictorian, class of 1936.**

This picture of Miss Oleson . . . I don't know when it was taken, but it looks just the way we remember she looked more than forty years ago. She was the librarian in Parley Grove, and she *looked* like the librarian. She seemed old even *then*. Maybe the way she wore her gray-streaked blond hair in a tight braid around a flat bun on the back of her head was just old-fashioned.

When we were kids, we figured Miss Oleson needed that bun on the back to balance the beak on the front. The Lord blessed Miss Oleson with a sturdy nose. It was a hearty nose. It was a robust nose. It was a strong nose. It was a nose she could have used as a bottle opener. It was actually her father's nose—Lars's nose. It hadn't looked that good on *him*. And it fit even worse on *her*. But it was one of the few things he left her that she still had: the nose and the last name and the house where she lived for most of her ninety years.

Svena is a Danish name that means "little swan." When Svena was a girl, she had golden hair that she wore in ringlets. She had blue, blue eyes—eyes that always laughed—and a turned-up smile. Back in those days, her nose was just a little button. She was the joy of the Oleson family, the only girl after eleven boys. She made her mother so happy. Axelina always wanted a girl. And they'd waited a long time for her, the Olesons had.

Her parents, Lars M. and Axelina Bergeson Oleson, were married in 1895. The boys started arriving in 1896, one every couple of years or so. The oldest was Soren, then Valgard. He was killed in Belgium. Then Gunnar and Meldun and Ivar and Vermund, Harold and Hjalmar, Jens, and Kylan, and finally Neil, who died when he was a baby. Axelina was into her forties by then. And they figured Neil was their last. But, four more years went by, and Svena came to their home as a happy surprise. It was good news.

This little girl grew up around a lot of men—big country men who were rough around the edges. But they doted on her. They spoiled her. And with her mother's help, she was all girl—all lace and curls and talcum powder. Axelina put Svena in the frilliest dresses she could sew. Little Svena was a flirt and a tease.

Her father, Lars, was president of the Taylor Stake for seventeen years. And when Svena was five or six, he sometimes took her on his church visits to show her off, she was such a pretty thing. He knew that he cut a stern figure himself, and he hoped she would make him more approachable.

In 1925, Elder David O. McKay came to Parley Grove as the presiding authority for the quarterly conference of the Taylor Stake. He stayed with the Olesons, in their home, for three nights. He was such a handsome man, Elder McKay. Fifty-two years old, a full head of almost snow-white hair. A dashing man who recited Burns and Wordsworth and Tennyson in the Oleson's parlor; a magnetic man who joined them in holding hands around the table in prayer. After supper, he opened a box of candy that he brought, and he gave Svena the first piece. Lars asked Brother McKay if he would like to hear Svena sing a song. Of course, he would. Anybody would want to be entertained by this beautiful child. And so Svena, six years old, sang "In Our Lovely Deseret" with its "Hark, Hark, Hark, 'tis children's music, children's voices, oh, how sweet!"

This was turning into a little family program for Elder McKay, who was so warm and so kind. Somebody cranked up the Victrola, and music from a record filled the parlor. It was a waltz. Svena was half hiding behind the armchair, and she gave Elder McKay a practiced wink. He winked back, and then he said, "Young lady, may I have the pleasure of this dance?"

And there in the parlor, little Svena Oleson reached up to hold the hands of Elder David O. McKay—that handsome man, that good and kind and cultured man—who twirled her around the floor to the scratchy recording of "Alice Blue Gown." It was one of those moments that you want to freeze and keep. And Svena kept that moment in her heart forever.

But now, eight decades later, she was taking a long time to die. She was going about it very slowly and not on anybody else's schedule. Every day Ralphene had arranged for women to sit with her—to fix her meals, to clean the old house, to take her to the clinic. Of course, nobody did more for her than Ralphene herself. And they've been close, the two of them. They've been close. Svena was Kanyon's great-aunt on his mother's side. Most of Svena's other relations have moved away. About a dozen years ago, Kanyon and Ralphene drove Svena and their kids up to Yellowstone. Oh, she loved it! She saw Old Faithful, she saw the bison, she saw Morning Glory Pool, she saw the falls, she even saw a bear. It was her first trip ever out of the state. She had the best time then! But lately, she was having such a hard time dying.

It wasn't like Ralphene had nothing else to do besides wait for Svena to go, because her daughter Charnelle was getting married on the 15th. Ralphene had so much to worry about, with the dress, and the flowers, and the invitations . . . with the reception, and the refreshments, and the dinner before. There was so much to think about, and Ralphene was exhausted. For the last few weeks she just hadn't felt herself.

It's a sensitive time when a mother's daughter gets married. It's a sensitive time. The mother relives her *own* wedding. That her *daughter* is doing this now makes the mother feel young again, and yet so old—all at the same time. The mother wants her daughter's wedding reception to be perfect, and she uses this reception to correct all the mistakes that were made in her own. And she remembers every one. The mother wants her daughter's wedding to be even nicer than hers was.

This was going to be a challenge for Ralphene, because she would be putting on this reception in Parley Grove, and Ralphene was not originally from a small town. No, Ralphene grew up in a much bigger, more sophisticated place. Ralphene grew up in Spanish Fork. They have caterers and bridal stores and florists and reception centers all in the yellow pages of the phone book there. There's none of that anywhere *near* Parley Grove. But, Parley Grove is where Ralphene has made her home for twenty-three years, ever since she married Kanyon. She's worked hard to fit in, to adapt to this place. But, even now, some of the older people still call her "Kanyon's wife." She knows she's not a native, and never will be.

But she is the Relief Society president and she does have charity. And she has the church gym for the reception. The proper term now is "cultural hall," but when they built Parley Grove's brick church fifty years ago, they called it what it was. So the wedding reception would be in the church gym, and the dinner before the reception would be in the church basement, and Ralphene was so worried the groom's family—the Williamses—might think the Hedbergs were hicks, because the Williamses were from Cedar City and both worked at the college.

The days before the wedding just flew by, and Ralphene wished she weren't so tired. If she just had a little more energy, and just a little more time, *maybe* she could make this wedding day and reception what she wished it could be.

Sometimes Ralphene talked about the wedding with Svena, to make conversation during the long hours she sat with her. One day Svena said, "It's not fair you should have to worry about your daughter's wedding and my funeral all at the same time."

Ralphene said, "Oh, Svena! I'm not planning your funeral!"

Svena said, "No, you're *not*. It's all ready. It's written out on a paper there in the bureau drawer. When I'm gone, you'll know where to find it. Give it to Bishop Thaxton. Tell him it's what I want. And don't let him change it. Don't let him change *a thing*."

And then she confided to Ralphene a secret—a dark secret with an explanation that someone, someday would need to know. The confession of a dying woman is something you have to respect, especially if you are the Relief Society president. And this Relief Society president would soon have to carry her own unspeakable secret to the old woman's grave. Two women bound by secrets.

Svena said, "And my obituary's in there, too. All ready. Have 'em print it in the weekly just the way it's written."

Svena had read nearly every book there ever was in Parley Grove—every book that came through her library, including one on thanatology, the study of dying. It said people ought to make plans for their dying, so they can get on with their lives. And Svena did that. She planned her own funeral; a *scandalous* funeral, I've heard some people say. There's never been a funeral like it in Parley Grove, *ever*. Until last week. And Svena planned it all, and wrote it all down, at the same time she wrote her obituary, months and months ago.

All those many years ago, when Svena was eleven, her mother died. It was pneumonia. Lars and the three boys still at home looked to Svena to keep up the house. She cooked the meals, did the laundry, bottled the fruit. She outgrew the frilly dresses her mother had made and new ones did not come. As the rest of Svena started to grow into a woman, she started to grow the nose of a man. Once that nose started to grow, it didn't quit. She looked just like her father. It was one of nature's cruel tricks that this child, who began as a beautiful little swan, should grow into an ugly duckling.

She survived high school by burying herself in books. She was relieved when school was over. But if you lived in Parley Grove in 1936, you didn't have a lot of places to go. And Lars depended on her; he couldn't manage alone. So she stayed with him; she cared for her father into his old age 'til he died in 1942. And the day after his funeral, Svena left town.

She got a job in Marysvale, working as a maid and a clerk at the old Grand Hotel and Boarding House. A lot of men were passing through in those days, mostly younger than she was—boys who'd come up from southern Utah and the Arizona strip to get on the train and go off to war. They were filled with their own dreams and fears and didn't pay Svena much attention. She blended into the background. It was a job. She was away, and on her own, and that was all.

Then one October afternoon Svena was at the front desk when a man in uniform came in. He said, "Excuse me, Miss. I'm lookin' for a room. Have you got a vacancy here?"

She replied, "Yes, we have a vacancy."

She got him registered.

He was a bit older than most of the men who came through. She told him what time dinner was served. Told him what time the train left for Salt Lake the next day. He was not an especially handsome man, but seemed to be a sensitive man. He had just finished officer training and had spent a week's leave at home before shipping out. He was a second lieutenant.

She told him the pool hall across the street was open until ten and the picture show in town was at eight. Breakfast in the morning was at seven.

He said, "Thank you, Miss—"

"Oh," she said, "Oleson. It's Svena Oleson."

He said "Svena?! Svena? *Really?* My *mother's* name is Svena. I thought she was the only one."

"No," Svena said.

The lieutenant said, "You must be Danish."

Svena said, "Yes. Both sides."

He said, "I sure wish you could meet my mother. She's in Fredonia."

Svena said, "Oh, I've never been there."

He said, "You should see it! You should visit my mother."

Svena said, "Oh, I don't know."

He said, "I can't *believe* this. Yesterday, when I told her goodbye, I had this terrible thought that I'd never see anybody named Svena again. But I was wrong, wasn't I? Because, already, I've met *you.*"

"Yes," Svena said.

He said, "Did you know that *Svena* means 'little swan'?"

"Yes," she said.

The lieutenant said, "Say, why don't you come with me to the movie tonight?"

"Oh," Svena said. "I—I don't—I don't get off work until eight."

He said, "Well, then we'll just miss the newsreel."

"Well, I, uh—I—"

"Eight o'clock," he said, "I'll meet you right here."

It was *Buck Privates,* a silly movie starring Abbott and Costello and the Andrews Sisters. Svena tried to laugh at it, but she was too nervous. He had paid for her ticket, and for a popcorn, too. And so she was almost certain that *this* was a *date.*

At the front desk of the hotel afterward, he told her it had been a swell time.

"Yes," Svena said.

He said, "I thought I knew the only Svena in the world. And today I met you."

"Yes," Svena said.

He said, "Here's my address—my mother's address. At least you could write her. I guess you could even write *me.*"

"Yes," Svena said.

He shook her hand.

Svena took three weeks to compose the letter—to get every word just right. She folded it in a Hallmark Christmas card she bought for fifteen cents, and she mailed it to the lieutenant in care of the address in Fredonia. In large letters, on the envelope, she wrote *PLEASE FORWARD.*

Svena stayed in Marysvale for another two and a half years. She watched for a reply in the mail every day she was there. And when the war was over, when she went home to Parley Grove, she watched for it there.

Last week, Svena's timing could not have been worse. When she finally died it was late Monday night, almost Tuesday. Bishop Thaxton had to break the news to Ralphene—the news about the schedule. He knew the wedding was Thursday. So the *funeral* would have to be Friday, which put the viewing on Thursday night, the same night as the wedding reception. Ralphene listened, and she saw her dreams for her daughter's perfect wedding day melt away. She said, "Bishop, couldn't the funeral wait until Saturday?"

Bishop Thaxton said, "It *could*. Any *other* week it could. But *this* Saturday's the deer hunt. We can't put people in a position like that."

And, of course, you couldn't.

Ralphene sustains authority. She has learned to carry on without complaint. So she asked how many would come to the funeral dinner the Relief Society would prepare. And she hung up. Then she started to cry. This meant Thursday night, the old brick church would be double-booked, with both the reception and the viewing—the happiest night of her daughter's life sharing the spotlight with an old woman's casket.

Both events would take place at the ward meetinghouse Thursday night. The funeral would follow on Friday.

People are *still* talking about that funeral. Based on Svena's written instructions, Bishop Leland D. Thaxton knew it was gonna be an outlandish funeral for Parley Grove, and it made him nervous. But he checked the handbook. He checked it twice. It didn't say you *couldn't* do it that way, and it's what Svena had written down that she wanted.

Ralphene was doing her best just to hold it together. She handed off as much of the funeral work as she could to her counselors, Devera and Trudell. Trudell said, "Now, you just enjoy the wedding and don't you worry about a thing." But by *this* time, Ralphene feared she had plenty to be worried about.

Charnelle was married in Manti. It was a beautiful ceremony. Ralphene cried through the whole thing. Charnelle asked, "Aren't you happy, Mother?"

Ralphene said, "Yes, of course, my baby—I'm happy." And she tried to make herself believe it was true.

After they lined up for pictures outside the temple, Ralphene made Kanyon stop at Manti Drug before they drove back to Parley Grove. She said, "I'm just feeling a little queasy. I need some Pepto-Bismol, and I'll be fine." Well, Pepto-Bismol wasn't going to cure what Ralphene was feeling. And it wasn't all she bought.

Back in the basement of Parley Grove's brick church, the Relief Society had an early dinner all ready for the wedding party—the Hedbergs of Parley Grove and the Williamses of Cedar City, and all the uncles and the aunts and the grandparents and the friends of the bride and the friends of the groom. And all of them were hungry after so much joy. And *such* a dinner! They served glazed ham and a kind of au gratin potatoes—a favorite wedding recipe where the potatoes are grated, then laced and baked with butter and melted cheese and topped with corn flake crumbs. They had Jell-O topped with Miracle Whip, and a tossed salad, and hot buttered rolls, and a frog-eye salad, and peas and corn—and for dessert, they had chocolate crunch cake with Cool Whip on top, and apple cider to drink. It was a *beautiful* dinner, and it was over by four.

The reception started at 6:30 there in the church. In the gym. The viewing in the Relief Society room started at the same time.

Actually, it worked out okay. It was a two-for-one night for most people. If you were going to one, you were going to the other, and you didn't have to get dressed up twice. You came and you stood in line in the gym—a long line that didn't move very fast, a line that eventually took you to another line of people who stood in front of some nice flowers and who each shook your hand and who thanked you for coming.

And you said you were happy for them, and isn't it wonderful for these occasions that bring us together? They're what life's all about. And you moved down the line, toward the star of the show, toward that girl in her special white dress, and you said how beautiful she looked—she never looked more beautiful than she did today. And all the way down that line, in the old brick church, you never guessed the deep secret that someone was hiding behind her brave smile—you never would have guessed that on this wedding day, this day of virtue and holiness, standing in the line, the bride's *mother* was pregnant!

Ralphene had confirmed it, with the test, just an hour earlier. She hadn't even told Kanyon. This was *Charnelle's* day. Ralphene would think about how she felt about the pregnancy tomorrow. First, she would get through today. She is a self-reliant woman. She will manage. She will be fine. Once she gets through today.

After you got through the wedding line, you sat down at a round table for eight, where a girl brought you a brownie and a nut cup and a lemonade spiked with Sprite. You polished that off, visited some with your neighbors, got up, and went toward the Relief Society Room to stand in another line.

Once again, you stood in a long line that didn't move very fast—a line that eventually took you to *another* line of people who stood in front of some nice flowers, and who each shook your hand and who thanked you for coming.

And you said you were happy for them, really, because it was her time, and isn't it wonderful for these occasions that bring us together? They're what life is all about. And you moved down the line toward the star of the show, that lady in her special white dress, and you said how beautiful she looked—she never looked more beautiful than she did today. Last week, when she was alive, she looked awful. She looked like death! Now she's dead, and she looks great. And all the way down that line, you never would have guessed the secret plot Svena had laid for the funeral tomorrow—the powerful statement that quiet woman would make to the world from inside her casket. This had never happened before at a funeral in Parley Grove. Never before, and maybe never again. Everybody's still talking about it.

It was the *pall bearers*. The pall bearers—Utahna Ovard, Sherma Belcher, Velta Crump, Dorsie Odle, VerJean Soderstrom, Oreta Horsley, NonaRene Nelford, and Ralphene Hedberg—were all *women!* All of the pall bearers were *women*, and most of 'em *old* women at that. Svena had confided her secret to Ralphene before she died. She said, "No man in Parley Grove ever took me out once in my whole life. And I'm *not* going to give them the pleasure of taking me out when I'm *dead.*"

So the funeral was Friday in the Parley Grove ward house, that old brick church, with Ralphene and seven other women carrying Svena out the door.

Ralphene hurried back from the cemetery to supervise the meal for family who'd come from out of town. Ralphene was there, the morning after her daughter's wedding, serving an early dinner and providing charity and relief with the rest of those good sisters, all of them motivated by love, and by duty, and by a little guilt.

And it was such a wonderful dinner! They served glazed ham, and a kind of au gratin potatoes—a favorite funeral recipe where the potatoes are grated, then laced and baked with butter and melted cheese and topped with corn flake crumbs. They had Jell-O topped with Miracle Whip, and a tossed salad, and hot buttered rolls, and a frog-eye salad, and peas, and corn—and, for dessert, they had chocolate crunch cake with Cool Whip on top, and apple cider to drink. It was a *beautiful* dinner.

Ralphene still wasn't ready to make the announcement on Friday. There'd be time. There'd be a time soon enough.

And soon enough, in maybe nine months or ten, a crowd will return to that old brick church—the building at the center of so much of their lives—for one of those wonderful occasions that bring us together. They are what life is all about. And—*assuming it's a girl*—the star of the show in the meetinghouse *that* day will be wearing *her* special white dress, and Kanyon will hold her up high, in front of the congregation, and they'll sigh a little bit, and they'll give a nervous chuckle, and they'll say how beautiful she looks. No baby girl will have ever looked more beautiful than she will on that day. And there'll be a lot of people who'll come. And there'll be a big dinner afterwards. And they'll probably serve funeral potatoes. It'll be good news, as soon as Ralphene is ready to share it.

But, that's getting ahead. I should read you the rest of the obituary that Svena wrote:

> **Svena Oleson lived a rich and full life, all but three years in Parley Grove. She loved to travel and visit new places. She traveled to places like Yellowstone National Park and Jackson Hole. She traveled to Idaho, Montana, and Wyoming, in addition to numerous trips to Salt Lake City. Through the pages of books, she visited even farther corners of the world. She loved corresponding with her many grand-nieces and -nephews. She attended a performance of Handel's *Messiah* in the Salt Lake Tabernacle. She loved music, and she loved to dance. And once she danced with David O. McKay.**

Part of that story's in the hometown weekly, the good news newspaper that helps you remember who you are and where you're from.

THE
PARLEY'S PROGRESS

SERVING PARLEY GROVE, UTAH'S 87TH LARGEST CITY, AND ALL OF TAYLOR COUNTY

GAMES OF CHANCE

The hometown weekly just came in the mail. This week in Out 'N About, EvaDean Thiede says:

> April showers that came our way
> have brought the dandelions of May.

Then she reports that Ida Mae Ipson, surrounded by her posterity, danced the Hokey Pokey for 'em all on her ninety-fourth birthday, and it was a wonder to behold!

On the front page, there is a picture of people standing around a cake, under the headline:

THIRTY-FIVE YEARS FOR TOLLEY AT PG PO

> Special to the Progress: Parley Grove Postmaster Effel Tolley last week celebrated thirty-five years on the job. Friends made it a party with a cake with frosting that said *Special Delivery Girl.*

That's a nice sentiment. Because now, thirty-five years later, Effel looks a little less like special delivery and a little more like bulk mail.

She holds a powerful position, Effel does—postmaster for Parley Grove. It means she's got the goods on everybody, knows stuff even Bishop Thaxton never finds out. Stuff like who gets tax refunds. Who gets past-due notices from the phone company. Who's mail-ordering stuff and where they get it and what it is, if she can possibly tell. Knows who's on the mailing list for the Victoria's Secret catalog, which Effel has seen, so she knows Victoria doesn't *have* any secrets. Not any more. The thing isn't sealed, so it's not as if she was snooping. It just sort of fell open. Effel *never* opens other people's mail—*sealed* mail, first-class mail. That's against the law. And Effel's a stickler for the law. But she does have an awfully bright lamp there in the back room. And if you hold an envelope up in its general vicinity, its contents *might* be visible. Accidentally, of course. Effel is the Parley Grove CIA, because the U.S. mail in Parley Grove—every piece of it—comes under her surveillance, and she keeps good track of it, coming in and going out, including *The Progress,* every week. So congratulations to Effel on thirty-five years.

The *big* headline in *The Progress* this week:

TOP ENTERTAINERS NAMED FOR PARLEYBRATION DAYZ

Parley Grove is pretty excited about this. It's a sign that Parleybration Dayz is rising to a whole new level, with a concert on opening night by real performers who get paid.

The story says:

> **Announced last Wednesday by the Parleybration Dayz Committee was the engagement of the popular Osguthorpe Brothers for an exclusive performance on Parleybration opening night. They will appear in concert at the Parley Grove rodeo arena on Friday, August 21st.**
>
> **Tickets are $4.00 in advance, $5.50 at the door.**

The Osguthorpe Brothers! An amazing group. Entertainers with real staying power. These guys have been performing together for nearly fifty years—Dalyn and Daryl and Ray and Maynard Osguthorpe.

And their younger brother, Duwanny, was a *solo* act for a while.

The Osguthorpes even made records! Back in their heyday they made a few 45s and one LP. They've been on tour through places like Wyoming and southern Idaho, and every county in Utah except for six. And in 1973 they performed in the lounge of Cactus Pete's in Jackpot, Nevada, for a whole entire week.

So these guys have really been around. They've been the headline performers at Spanish Fork Onion Days, at Leamerado (in Leamington), and at the Panguitch rodeo.

The Osguthorpes!

And they *could* have been even bigger—the Osguthorpes could have been *world*-famous—if they'd just had a fair shot on their television debut back . . . back . . . *way* back in the early 1960s. It was a show in Salt Lake— Eugene Jelesnik's *Talent Showcase,* kind of a local, early version of *American Idol*.

But being from Paragonah, the Osguthorpe Brothers were at an unfair disadvantage from the start on this show—the *same* show, *as chance would have it*—on the *same week* that the Osmond Brothers made *their* television debut. Because the Osmond Brothers were from Ogden, which is a *big city*.

So the cards were stacked against the Osguthorpes from Paragonah when it came to the call-in voting, even though *they* sang barbershop just like the Osmonds did. And while they sang, the Osguthorpes accompanied themselves on an accordion, a washboard, a Jew's harp, and a saw. And while they sang and accompanied themselves, they *clogged,* all at the same time!

To this day, some of their fans think that if the voting had been fair, the Osguthorpes would have gone on to Disneyland and the *Andy Williams Show,* on to fame and fortune and a theater in Branson, and the Osmonds would still be singing at Wheat and Beet Days in Tremonton. But that's not how luck had it.

Still, the Osguthorpe Brothers' fans are loyal. And *Southern Utah Entertainment Quarterly* in its first (and final) issue recognized the Osguthorpes as "a truly homegrown phenomenon."

And to their credit, the Osguthorpe Brothers have never let fame go to their heads, and they never became bitter over not being the biggest commercial success. They know life isn't always fair, and part of it is chance, and they've moved past that. A few of their hard-core fans, though, have suspicions to this day that the Osmonds stole some of the Osguthorpe's material. The fans love hearing the Osguthorpe Brothers sing their old hits like "One Bad Apricot" and "Down by the Crazy River" and "She Ain't Heavy, She's My Mother." They notice that the Osmonds had some songs with very *similar* lyrics, and they suspect there might have been foul play. I don't know.

But even if the Osguthorpes *were* cheated out of first prize on Eugene Jelesnik's *Talent Showcase,* and even if they never could afford braces to have teeth like the Osmonds' teeth, well, they have never complained. Even now—even while age is taking its toll, and they can't clog quite like they used to, and they don't break-dance any more—they keep faith with their loyal fans. They still travel around the state in their Ford Econoline van, and sing—with their karaoke machine and their minus tracks—at county fairs and firesides and grand openings of WalMart. And the good news is they will be in Parley Grove this summer, August 21st, for Parleybration Dayz, and that'll really be something. And you are all invited.

Cloby Stubsted was volunteered to head up the raffle this year at Parleybration Dayz. They usually raffle off a dirt bike or a four-wheeler or a nice rifle—a raffle rifle—or something like that as the grand prize, with a bunch of smaller prizes on the side. They wanted Cloby to handle that this year. People have been putting a little more stock in Cloby ever since he got called to the high council. And so, just last week, the committee asked him to be in charge of this year's raffle.

But he told 'em no. He turned them down flat. Which was a surprise, because Cloby's a sweet man, and he would do just about anything anybody asked him to do, *except commit sin*. He's such a straight arrow now—been tryin' to hold to the rod ever since his new call—and has faithfully filled his high council assignment, which has mostly been to keep the old furnace at the church house in West Dip working.

Changed man that he is, Cloby has resolved never to return to his follies. He's dealing with enough guilt right now over what was really just an unintended transgression. But he thinks President Markum has found him out. Why else would he have assigned Cloby to give a talk on the very vice that snared him? And then, how could Cloby be such a hypocrite as to give that talk and then turn around and run the raffle?

Giving the talk is guilt enough. It's coming up two weeks from Sunday. Cloby's first high council talk. He's been on the council now for nearly six months, and President RDell C. Markum has put off having him speak for about as long as he could. And how that talk's gonna go in two weeks, heaven only knows.

Cloby has been agonizing over it for nearly two weeks already, which is probably more preparation than the rest of the high council collectively has spent on all their talks this year. This month's topic is clear and direct. President Markum has been concerned about it ever since he heard what happened with some of the Saints from Taylor County over spring break.

The whole idea of spring break is still causing a fuss in Parley Grove. The Taylor County School District started it just a couple of years ago, caving in to what people are doing in the cities. And we know it's a foolish thing to try to be like everybody else. Spring break was not part of our tradition. There's no history or reason behind it, like there is for fall recess, which is for the deer hunt. Some people think spring break's just an excuse to get into trouble. And there is suspicion that this year, some people actually *did*. Some people who you'd think would have better things to do put their kids in the car, left town, and headed south—*south,* to warmth and sunshine, which can lead to all sorts of temptation. Man was not intended to take off his coat so early in the year.

And when some of those people got to St. George, they didn't stop. No! They kept right on going all the way to Mesquite! In *Nevada!* And they weren't going *there* to see relatives. We know that. Doyce Hickel said it was just that motel rooms were cheaper in Mesquite than they were in St. George. Well, if that's true, you *know* it's because of the money those motels—those *casinos*—take in from gambling.

It's easy to rationalize, to make excuses about vice—that monster of awful mien, since first we endure, then pity, then embrace. And Cloby plans to use that poem in his talk, by the way. But he won't be self-righteous about it. That's not in his soul. He is totally repentant. In fact, he would show up in sackcloth and ashes to give that talk if he hadn't already bought his high council blue suit. He'd wear sackcloth and ashes, because he feels such remorse now that he knows the doctrine.

He knows it *now*. But he didn't just three weeks ago Saturday when Chlorine brought home the mail and said there was an envelope for him.

A big envelope stamped *Important Notice.* Big envelope. All the way from Port Washington, New York. It said *Open Immediately: Documentation response requested. Material enclosed intended solely for addressee.* And the addressee was Clobert T. Stubsted. Big envelope. Looked *very* important.

Cloby sat down at the kitchen table and opened the pen knife on his janitor key ring. He unsealed that big envelope, sliced it carefully along the top.

Inside, it was full of certificates and documents and a letter addressed to him. Some of the stuff in pretty fine print.

Cloby said, "Where's my glasses, Mother?"

Chlorine brought him his glasses from where he'd left them, on top of *Especially For Mormons,* Volume Five, which is also coming in handy for his talk.

Cloby adjusted his glasses and started reading the personal letter to him from a Dave Sawyer, who said he wanted to give Cloby a million dollars!

Instructions for Mr. Clobert T. Stubsted: Do not delay. The winning number could be in your hands right now. Make sure to enter your valid number in the winning range by completing the enclosed instructions.

Well, those instructions were about as long and about as clear as the ones from the IRS, and Cloby knew this could take him some time. So he got up and went to the cupboard and sliced himself a piece of bread and slathered it with margarine and apple jelly, and he poured himself a glass of milk—something to give him the energy to get through this and figure it out. He wasn't sure why Dave Sawyer wanted to give him a million dollars; wasn't even sure who Dave Sawyer was. But Cloby sat back down at the table with his bread and jelly and glass of whole milk, and his certificates and documents, and he put on his glasses and approached this as methodically as he could.

Eventually, Cloby mostly figured it out. He figured out that this was not exactly a *promise* that Dave would send him a million dollars; he wasn't there just yet. First, Dave was sending him the Super Prize Number that was *probably* the one for the million dollars. Dave *thought* it was, but he couldn't be sure—couldn't be sure until Cloby sent that number back in. And Dave needed Mr. Clobert T. Stubsted to paste his valid Super Prize Number label in one square, and the label saying he understood that the prizes were actually awarded in another square, and the local award stamp in a third square saying he understood that a major prize of at least one thousand dollars would be awarded to somebody in the state of Utah. And those stamps were sort of hidden in a whole sheet of stamps for magazines, more or less in alphabetical order. This was a lot to think about.

There was another sheet listing the other amazing prizes Dave had to give away. That was his job, he wrote, as the executive director of the Prize Patrol. And he included for Cloby his business card with his personal telephone number, in case Cloby had any questions. Well, Cloby was sure he could figure this out by himself. Dave Sawyer was probably a busy man, and this was Saturday, and besides, to call him would be long distance.

Well, it took some time—actually, about an hour and a half—but Cloby found those three stamps Dave was looking for, and he pasted them in there. And then, down at the bottom of the page were more squares where Cloby could put stamps for magazines, *if he wanted to.*

Cloby looked through that page of stamps again. A lot of magazines he'd never heard of. He found *Ebony* and *Entertainment* and *Essence* and *ESPN the Magazine,* but he couldn't find the *Ensign,* which was the one magazine he knew Chlorine took.

He wondered if it made any difference to Dave whether he ordered a magazine. Cloby probably wouldn't have been so concerned about that if he hadn't seen, as he went through the pages again, the other prizes Dave said he had to give away—in addition to the Super Prize of one million dollars. Dave had five Grand Prizes to give away, too: the winner's choice of five luxury vehicles. And one of them was a Winnebago. Oh! Cloby has dreamed for thirty years of owning a Winnebago . . . something he and Chlorine could just jump in and go to places he'd never been—go first-class to places like Idaho. And cities he's never been to—cities with exotic names like Pocatello or Winnemucca or Walla Walla. Or, if he got really brave, all the way to Cheektowaga—faraway places with strange-sounding names.

He and Chlorine could go to places like that and stay at an RV park, hook up to the water and the power and just stay there in style as long as they felt like it, and have just a nifty retirement checking out Winnemucca in his Winnebago. Cloby's been saving up for it, just not very fast. And he always figured he'd buy a *used* Winnebago if his dream ever came true. But Dave Sawyer was talking about a brand-new Winnebago. And though it probably wouldn't be fitting to be a millionaire—not that Cloby had ever given much thought to that—he *could* see himself driving that Winnebago, and Dave could give the million to somebody else. That'd be fair enough.

Cloby was starting to get a little excited about this, and thought he ought to get a second opinion from some of the boys. Some of them do a Saturday lunch down to the ChatNChew. So he took the truck into town, pulled up to the place, and found Vernus and Buzz and Cleelan and Wink all at the counter. Athlene said, "Chili's good today, Cloby," and Cloby ordered a bowl of chili and a Coke, and he told the boys about the Winnebago and his letter from Dave.

He said, "Probly, though, ain't one chance in ten I got the real number."

Cleelan said, "More like one 'na hunerd."

And Vernus said, "Well, I'll tell you this: If you *don't* send 'er in, yer chance is flat-out zero!"

And Buzz said, "Now there's a truth." Which seemed to Cloby to be the most persuasive argument there was.

He said, "So, think I oughta' send 'er in?"

Buzz said, "My wife gits 'em and sends 'em in all the time. And she's still waitin' on the prize."

"Does she order from 'em?" Cloby asked. "Does she buy the magazines?"

"Don't make no difference for winnin'," Buzz said. "That's the law. So do what ya want."

Well, when Cloby looked over the stamps again, he figured he had no use for *American Artist* or *Arthritis Today* or *Architectural Digest*—or pretty much the rest of 'em, so he decided to send Dave just the three stamps he needed, and not order any magazines *at this time.* That's what Cloby resolved to do, and he stopped at the post office on the way home, late Saturday afternoon. He invested forty-two cents in a postage stamp from the machine, and before he dropped the envelope into the slot, he drew on the little sheet Dave had sent him to diagram where, exactly, his house was, in case they needed to find it to put him on live TV in the middle of the *NBC Nightly News* on August 21st as the winner of the big prize. Since Cloby's never liked to be in the spotlight, that was another reason to hope for the Winnebago and not the million dollars. But he sealed the envelope and licked the stamp and dropped it in the slot.

That was on a Saturday.

Sunday, the high council got the topic for their next talk: *the evils of gambling and games of chance.* Cloby looked up "games of chance" in *Mormon Doctrine.* It said, "See gambling." And right there on the opposite page, under Gambling, he read the doctrine: *Whether called games of chance, something for nothing, or by any other name, gambling is gambling and is a pernicious evil.* And we all know that it is!

That was Sunday.

Monday morning, Cloby unlocked the high school early, got back in his truck, and drove over to the post office. He waited out front until Effel Tolley showed up to open the place at 7:30—Effel Tolley, who's ruled over this little corner of a branch of the federal government for thirty-five years.

She said, "Mornin', Cloby. You're here early."

He said, "Mornin', Effel," which is about all the conversation she would have expected from Cloby. But he said more. He said, "I was thinkin' you might could help me out."

"Well," she said, "just give me two shakes, and I'll have this place open. Got somethin' to mail?"

"Nope," Cloby said. "Already done it."

"All right, then, whaddaya need?"

Cloby said, "See, Saturday, after you was closed, I mailed a letter."

"Okay," Effel said.

"And I changed my mind."

"Changed your mind?"

"It was a mistake," Cloby said. "I don't want to send 'er no more. I want 'er back. Can I have 'er back?"

This sounded pretty juicy to Effel for so early on a Monday morning. She asked, "What *was* it?" as if the answer might make a difference.

Cloby said, "It was—well, it was just a letter." He saw no need to go into particulars.

Effel went behind the counter and over to the mail slot. She picked up the plastic bin that held the weekend's deposits. She couldn't wait to hear Cloby's story. She put the bin on the counter.

"Well, Cloby, there's all sorts of letters in here. I suppose yours would have your return address."

"Well, no," Cloby said. "I don't think she did."

"Cloby, you should put a return address on every piece of your mail," Effel said. She made it sound more like a regulation than a leg up for her snooping. "And if your name isn't on it, how could you prove it's yours?"

"Well, I'd reco'nize 'er."

"And *how* would you recognize it, Cloby? What makes it distinctive?" Effel's line of questioning was turning sharp.

"Well, I know who's I sent it to."

Effel moved in for the kill. "And who'd ya' send it *to?*"

Cloby had the vague sense Effel might be prying.

"Ain't that 'posed to be my *own* business?" he asked.

Effel said, "Suit yourself!" She picked up the bin and started to turn, with his folly in her grasp, about to make Cloby's indiscretion of the heart a transgression in the flesh.

Cloby said, "Confound it, Effel, I sent away to some fella who might could give me a Winnebago. Dave Sawyer, if ya have to know. But I don't want 'er no more. And I don't want a million dollars, and I don't want no magazines!"

Effel turned back toward him, and she winnowed through the pile of letters until she came to one preaddressed to Port Washington, New York. She gave it a look and looked at Cloby and then held it up.

"So, it's *this* one," she said. "Well, Cloby, there's no fool like an old fool." She dropped the envelope back in the bin and lifted it from the counter.

Cloby said, "Give 'er to me Effel! Come on. Give 'er here."

"Cloby Stubsted!" Effel said. "You know I can't give it back. It's been the property of the United States Postal Service ever since you dropped it in the slot. If I gave it to you I would be breaking the law."

A fairly condescending response from a woman who for thirty-five years has made it her business to know the business of everybody in town based on every piece of mail they ever sent or received. There must be some regulation about *that*. But she refused.

And just for an instant, a dark, fleeting thought passed through Cloby's mind. It was gone almost before it was there. But he's bigger than Effel. He could just—

Oh! It's a terrible thing how vice tempts you to cover your tracks, with more evil still. But Cloby stood fast against the thought. Which, of course, is good news.

He went out the door with his head down, and Effel went back to sorting through the bin. She found about fourteen more envelopes just like the one she pulled out for Cloby, all preaddressed to Port Washington, New York.

But what Cloby did is done. Now he's got to bear the shame of it while he prepares for his talk. That'll be a week from Sunday.

Then he's got three months to *keep* worrying until August 21st, when— *talk about having your sins shouted from the housetops*—when it could be announced to all the world in the middle of *NBC Nightly News,* that *Brother* Clobert T. Stubsted had played a game of chance. Played and *won,* if they announce it. Such public humiliation.

But Cloby's not gonna make it easy for that to happen. First of all, if Dave Sawyer comes looking for him on August 21st, Cloby won't be home. He's decided he'll be gone all day, until it gets dark, and then he'll be down to Parleybration Dayz—clappin' for the Osguthorpe Brothers from the back row, with his hat pulled down and his head kept low. And you can bet your mother he *won't* be running the raffle! *That* guilt can go to somebody else. Which is good news for Cloby.

Remember, you're all invited to the opening of Parleybration Dayz with the Osguthorpes on August 21st. I hope you can come. But if you can't, at least be sure to watch the *NBC Nightly News* that night so you can see how this whole thing turns out.

In the meantime, if there is a moral to this story—though personally, I don't recommend morals to stories—but if there *is* a moral, it might be this: *Steer clear of the vice of somethin' for nothing. Next* time, be sure to order a magazine from Dave. And then, if *he* decides he wants to send you a million dollars, or a Winnebago, that'll just be *his* business.

Part of that story's in the hometown weekly, the good news newspaper that helps you remember who you are and where you're from.

PARLEY'S PROGRESS

MATCHMAKER

The hometown weekly just came in the mail. The front-page headline, with lovely pictures to match:

FOUR VIE FOR MISS TAYLOR COUNTY

The pageant's in the high school auditorium this Saturday night. And it's the *big* one, the one that leads all the way to Miss *America*. So who knows? Miss America *could* come from Parley Grove. Might be one of these four. Just think about it. When I was in high school, Parley Grove had a State Dairy Princess First Runner-up. And, if—at any time, for any reason—the head Dairy Princess had not been able to fulfill her duties, it would have been our gal! We came awfully close.

These pageants don't seem to be quite as popular as they once were. Only four contestants this year, which is gonna make it hard when one gets to be Miss Taylor, two get to be the first or second counsel—uh, *attendants*, I guess it is—and one gets left out. Which is, I think, why they invented Miss Congeniality. But a beautiful girl is a beautiful girl.

The second page carries this week's somber news: Here's the obituary of one of the last of the real characters in Parley Grove. You hate to see him go. But the man was nearly a hundred, and sooner or later, we all have to answer the bell. May the rest of us die just as happy as Arzley Criddle did. Last week at the viewing there at the meetinghouse, he looked so peaceful—looked just like himself, just like he always did, behind that pair of thick glasses. And maybe *that's* why they left 'em on him, so he *would* look the same. Otherwise, glasses on a dead man don't make a lot of sense, do they? Glasses are the least of Arzley's worries now, with his eyes closed the way they are. And when they do open again, on that glorious morning, I can't imagine reading an eye chart is going to be a problem. Makes you wonder if whoever decided to bury him in glasses was lacking just a little faith. But, whatever the next life turns out to be like, Arzley would tell you he had a wonderful life here. In spite of how it started.

He was born in 1908, the last of the thirteen children of Zebulon and Zina Mercy Criddle. Arzley was the runt of the litter. The seven of his eight older brothers who lived all stood more than six-feet-two. Arzley was five-foot-four on his best day, and going bald by the eighth grade. A man's spirit may come from heaven, but his body seems to come from the luck of the draw. It's the gene pool jackpot. And Arzley's spirit did not hold the winning ticket. He got all the recessive genes. He had runny gray eyes that, through the thick glasses he wore, looked as big as biscuits. He had a bad leg from the time he was three and fell into a hole dug for the new privy. Even then, he could hardly see his hand in front of his face. But Arzley's eyesight was a disability that I would not make light of, even if some people back in those early days did.

You can understand why he would become the black sheep of the family. His parents were good people, Zeb and Zina Mercy were, but those were hard years in Parley Grove, and by the time Arzley came along, they were pretty well worn out. Those were the years when Zeb used to say if he had a million dollars, he'd just keep farming until it was all gone.

Well, Arzley left school just shy of his fifteenth birthday, having learned all he figured there was to know and having lost most of his hair. He just hung around the farm for a few years after that, and took up with a pretty sorry crowd—the other outcasts of the county. That meant the boys who smoked cedar bark, and sipped hard cider from Mason jars, and might have cussed a little while they played poker. And once, when a seedy carnival came through town, they each paid twenty-five cents to see some genuine French postcards. The postcards weren't a *huge* sin for Arzley, really, because with his eyes, he never could tell what the pictures were.

But he was *interested* in women. And in 1933 he went to the Parley Grove Deer Hunters Ball figuring to meet some, which he had no idea how to do. The girls were all standing together on one side of the hall. Arzley could tell they were the women, but he had to put *his* face right up to *their* faces to tell what they looked like and who they were—his eyes floating in those fish bowl glasses, staring at the girls from just inches away. Arzley limped down the line, squinting up into their faces, one at a time, to check 'em out.

He could see Laveen Prisbey's red hair clearly. It stood out. It looked nice. And she wasn't too tall.

"Let's shake a leg, Sister," he said to Laveen. "You look like one hot little number."

"Yeah, Arzley," Laveen said. "And you give me the heebee-jeebies. Scram, frog face, and I'll see *you* in a pig's eye."

The girls started to laugh. The whole line of them. Laveen, especially. They couldn't stop. Arzley just stood there; he didn't know what to say. Then Laveen stuck *her* nose right in front of *his* and said, "Beat it, you bug-eyed little hick." And they all laughed louder. Arzley Criddle looked down at his feet, and he hobbled out the side door at the same time the band started to play "Can This Be Love?" After that, nobody saw Arzley around Parley Grove for a long time.

He tried working in a sheep camp for a while, but with his eyes he couldn't tell the sheep on the hill from the rocks. So that didn't work out. Then he joined the CCC camp in Stibnite Canyon. Arzley was a good worker. But the showoffs and the bullies gave him a hard time, and he didn't fit in there. So he quit the CCC with nowhere to go and no direction in his life. Which is the reason that—as a last resort—he took old Shadrach up on his offer.

Shadrach Bendershot was a broken-down prospector from Arizona, still chasing the dream of striking it rich. That dream was about all Shadrach had. He had no home. Had no family, no friends, no faith. Just had a lot of old stories to tell, a lot of empty years, and a lot of bad luck. He had only that dream to give him a reason to live—that dream and a few mining claims in the canyon where he was looking for more. But he was too old and worn out to work the claims by himself, and he didn't have any money to hire a man. So what he proposed to Arzley was a deal: Shadrach would furnish the knowledge, or so he said, and Arzley would furnish the labor. And they would share the claims fifty-fifty, which shows you how desperate old Shadrach was.

That's how Arzley wound up living out there in that tumble-down cabin, listening every night to a half-crazy old man plot his revenge on fate—the revenge he'd have when they struck it rich. It was a dream that gave Shadrach more satisfaction than any riches ever could. Or ever would. Because he died three months into their partnership. And then Arzley just stayed out there by himself—still infected by the spirit of that bitter old man, becoming the closest thing to a hermit you'd ever see, which was a great and abiding sadness to his family.

The turning point in his life came with the quarterly Taylor Stake conference in May 1937. Not that Arzley went. But his father, Zeb, took the liberty of asking for a word with the visiting brother, Elder J. Golden Kimball. J. Golden was a legend in his time—a beloved man of God and a man of the people, which is what gave Zeb the courage to approach him;

that, and the fact that he was almost family, since Zina Mercy Criddle was the niece of Elder J. Golden Kimball's half-sister.

"What is it, Brother Criddle?" Elder Kimball asked.

Zeb said, "It's my boy." And before he knew it, he had poured out the full story and the sadness of his heart over his lost and lonely son.

Brother Kimball said, "What that boy of yours needs is a wife! A wife would straighten him out! That's mostly what done it for me."

Zeb said, "I know. But no woman would *have* Arzley. And you can't blame 'em for that."

"Horse feathers," J. Golden said. "There's sisters in the kingdom so desperate for a man they'd take a dead one. 'Specially some of them girls in Sanpete. Homely as gunny sacks—may the Lord have *mercy* on 'em. I can find a wife for your boy, Brother Criddle! You tell that son of yours that one of God's servants wants a word with him."

This was the plan: J. Golden was visiting a conference every week in May. At the end of the month, he would be at the Sevier Stake conference, which was not all that far from Parley Grove. He told Zeb to have Arzley meet him there, in Richfield, but not to tell Arzley what it was about.

Zeb said, "Yes, Brother Kimball. Thank you, Brother Kimball. I'll ask him. But I don't know that he'll come."

"'Course you don't *know*," J. Golden said. "The boy has agency. So tell him it's his *choice*. He can go to Richfield if he wants. Or, if he *wants*, he can go to hell!"

(Brother J. Golden *loved* to say "hell" when, like that, it *technically* wasn't swearing.)

Well, Zeb Criddle sent word to his son about the invitation to meet Brother Kimball—the generous and forceful invitation from one of the Brethren, who'd taken a personal interest in *him*. Arzley considered it for about two seconds, and then he said no. He was not going. He was too busy, all by himself, out there in the cabin. Truth be told, he had a *couple* of reasons for staying out there. As lonely as he was, he had pretty much given up on mixing with people. People had not made him happy. And second, he was out there, all by himself, trying to hide a secret. A secret can consume a man as much as a dream can. Only it's *worse*. Because a dream, at least, moves you forward. But a secret holds you back.

Not more than a week before that old prospector died, he found a vein of antimony in the canyon. It was so rich, so concentrated, that though it wasn't gold and it wasn't silver, it was good enough. Old Shadrach said they'd both be rich. He'd struck it rich, after all those years. He'd have everything that money could buy, and nothing that it can't. They went together to the courthouse in town, on the quiet, to file their claim.

When it was done, old Shadrach was feeling so good, he took out his last five-dollar gold piece and bought a bottle of whiskey to see him through the night. In the morning, they found Shadrach on the loading dock of the feed store, frozen stiff as a board, still holding the bottle. His leathery fingers clamped it so tight, the undertaker never could pry 'em loose. So he just buried old Shadrach with the whiskey bottle in his hand. I guess if you can bury a man with his glasses, you can bury him with his whiskey. The deed might have been a small comfort in death to a man who found so little comfort in life.

Well, old Shadrach's grave is up there in the cemetery to this day, and the teenagers still go there on Halloween.

But when Shadrach died, that meant the mining claims belonged to Arzley, free and clear. In the spring, he arranged to show 'em to an engineer, representing VMEC, the Volcanilium Minerals Extraction Corporation of McGill, Nevada.

The engineer looked over the claims and told Arzley he was sitting on the mother load of antimony. VMEC offered a deal: it would lease Arzley's claims for $9,000 up front cash and a 1 percent royalty on all minerals extracted there for thirty-five years. So Arzley had a secret: he was sitting on a pile of money! At least, he soon *would* be. And Arzley thought about money as his revenge against people. Not that he had a plan—all he had was a secret.

So he had no intention of going to Richfield to meet some Brother Kimball. Who he *was* going to see in Richfield was VMEC's attorney so he could sign the lease on his claims and get his $9,000 cash, which was a ton of money in Parley Grove in 1937. The attorney was in Richfield. And their appointment just happened to be two weeks from Friday, on the eve of the Sevier Stake conference. So the rest of this story could be coincidence, or it could be Providence. It's not for me to say.

Arzley stepped off the train at the little platform in Richfield and was trying to make out through his triple-thick glasses which way he ought to go, when somebody called, "Why, Arzley, ain't that you?" It was his Uncle Valno. Arzley hadn't seen Uncle Valno in eight or nine years, and he wasn't too happy to be seeing him now. Arzley might not have recognized *him*, but nobody could *not* recognize Arzley.

Uncle Valno was helping an old man on the platform who looked considerably overdressed. "Brother Kimball," Valno said, "this is my wife's sister's boy, Arzley Criddle. Quite a surprise he's here."

Then Valno—President Valno P. Worthy of the Sevier Stake—said, "Arzley, meet Brother J. Golden Kimball. He's come to preside at our conference."

Brother Kimball said, "God bless you for coming, boy. I *prayed* that you would."

Well, President Valno P. Worthy didn't know what that meant, and had no idea what he had done by insisting Arzley stay with *them*—which meant sharing the spare room with Brother Kimball that night. That would be after Arzley made his secret visit to the office of Boylynn Cloward, attorney at law.

The papers Mr. Cloward asked Arzley to sign ran to thirty-eight pages. Arzley insisted Cloward read every one of them to him, out loud, and then tell him what they meant. It took so long that by the time they finished, the bank had closed, and Arzley couldn't get his $9,000 out until Monday. That meant he'd have to stay in Richfield through the weekend to get that $9,000 in cold, hard cash. If he could have gotten the money, he wouldn't have stayed—or at least he would have stayed in a hotel. But as it was, he was at the mercy of his Uncle Valno.

And that's how it came to be that the very next night, Arzley Criddle met Dagmar Leudke.

They called her the quietest girl in Gunnison. She was too shy to say "boo" to a goose. Dagmar made noise only when she played the organ in church— and she did play the organ beautifully. Her three younger sisters—Brigitta, Solveig, and Kirsten—grew up and got married, and they married pretty well. Dagmar wanted to marry as much as any girl did, but she understood that *her* life was different. So she stayed busy with her handwork and her music and her books. She'd read every book in the Gunnison Library.

There were not a lot of prospects for a young woman like Dagmar in a place like Gunnison at a time like that. She *might* have been a beauty, like her sisters were. All of them were beautiful. Like them, Dagmar was tall and slender with red hair and blue eyes. But instead of looking at those blue eyes, people looked away. They always had, ever since she was four.

Her father was with the men branding cattle. Dagmar had fetched his canteen. She had filled it and was running to her father as fast as she could go, holding that canteen to her chest with both arms, the red curls bouncing behind her, when she tripped and fell head-first into the fire. It took years for the burns to heal, and when the bandages came off, she had no eyelashes and no eyebrows. The burns reshaped her features so that by the time she started school, the other kids called her names.

No, Dagmar had no marriage prospects in Gunnison—or in Fayette, or Mayfield, or Centerfield, or Sterling, or Axtell.

But she was playing the organ at the Gunnison Stake conference that May when J. Golden Kimball visited. And when he asked the local brethren about her, he had Zebulon Criddle's son in mind.

Brother J. Golden gave Dagmar a calling: to travel down to the Sevier Stake conference the following week and to play a special number on the organ there. They didn't have that kind of talent in Richfield, he told her. And he also wanted her to play the piano at the conference dance on Saturday night.

Well, Dagmar had never played music outside of Sanpete County. And she'd *never* been to a dance. But she was a faithful woman, and Brother Kimball had asked her, and so she went.

Arzley did not go to the Saturday conference dance willingly. He had been to a dance before. But when Brother J. Golden explained to President Valno P. Worthy what was at stake, Uncle Valno took Arzley by the ear and herded him to the dance and stood watch at the door so he couldn't leave.

Brother Kimball showed up for the intermission and spoke a few words to the crowd. He said they should seek wholesome entertainment, and they should shun the sin of tobacco—and he said they should be sure to attend the conference in the morning. And then he called on Dagmar Leudke, a visiting performer, for a special number. She didn't raise her eyes to anybody, but she sat down at the piano and played a tune she'd learned from the radio, "The Way You Look Tonight." It was lovely. Brother J. Golden cornered Arzley and said, "Son, that's one of God's choicest daughters playing that piano. I'm gonna introduce you. And if you have any brains in your head, you'll show that sister a good time." Arzley was sure he couldn't do that. And he was determined not to try.

But when the tune was over, Brother Kimball made introductions. "Sister Leudke, this is Brother Criddle. Brother Criddle, meet Sister Leudke." That was it. And it was awkward, as awkward as could be. Dagmar stood a full head taller than Arzley. He was twenty-nine, she was thirty-four. He was coarse, she was refined. With all due respect to Brother Kimball, they did not look like a match made in heaven.

Late that night, in Uncle—President—Valno P. Worthy's house, Brother Kimball waited up to ask Arzley what he thought of Sister Leudke.

"She ain't even pretty," Arzley said.

"Ain't pretty?!" J. Golden was shouting. "What does a man like you know about 'pretty'? Gimme those glasses." J. Golden pulled the glasses off Arzley's face and looked at them. "Good heavens, boy," he said. "No *wonder* you can't tell. You're blind as a bat! If you don't take my word for how beautiful she is, you deserve to live alone for the rest of your life.

"Squint your sorry eyes at her tomorrow, and look at her good," he said. "Because that face—that face—is the face of an angel. The most beautiful face in the world. And if you'da had a lick of sense in your head, you *could* have had her."

Keep in mind, Brother Kimball was eighty-four years old. Those were pretty strong words from an eighty-four-year-old man.

Brother Kimball handed Arzley back his glasses, then sat down on his bed.

"How the youth of Zion falter!" he said.

Then neither one of them said anything for a long time.

After a while Arzley said, "What do you mean I *could* have had her?"

By now, Brother J. Golden was ready for bed and out of patience. He said, "Forget it, 'cause I'm done with you. You couldn't afford her anyway, you sorry loafer."

That was pretty harsh judgment, coming from an eighty-four-year-old man who was tired and ready for bed!

He wasn't quite done. He said, "A beautiful woman like that would expect a diamond ring. And a *big* one! Soon as she found out how poor *you* are, she wouldn't waste a *minute* on you. Nor should she . . . beautiful, fancy woman like that."

And then came his final words on the subject. He said, "Any man lucky enough to win a woman like that would have to give every day of his life to showing her kindness and making her happy. That's what it takes, Brother Criddle. And I think you ain't up to it."

Pretty strong words. But Arzley heard them—every one of them. And to his credit, he remembered them.

Brother Kimball had worked his way into bed and put a pillow over his ears when he muttered that he was going to introduce her to some college boy up in Salt Lake—some fella who's smart and good-looking.

Arzley sat on his bed thinking it over for a long time. I don't believe he *meant* to say it out loud, but he *did*. He said to nobody in particular, "*I* got money. I got $9,000!"

Sometime that night, Arzley traded a secret for a dream.

Sunday morning in the Richfield Tabernacle he leaned over the balcony and squinted as hard as he could in the direction of the organ. Dagmar was playing a majestic arrangement of "Zion Stands With Hills Surrounded." There *was* something about her face, it seemed, that did set it apart. It wasn't just like all the rest. Arzley could tell. Brother Kimball must have been right.

Outside, after the conference, Arzley said, "Sister Leudke, you played beautiful music."

The woman said, "That's kind of you, Brother, but I'm Sister Sorensen."

When Dagmar *did* come out, he said it again: "Sister Leudke, you played beautiful music."

"Thank you," she said. "If you liked it, then I'm happy."

"Oh, Sister, Leudke, I *more* than liked it," he said. "It was, it was real—swell, Sister Leudke."

"Call me *Dagmar,*" she said.

And that's the way it began. The most unlikely relationship. Which just proves that for every Jack there is a Jill.

If they would have had sons, they would have named them Kimball or Golden, I'm quite sure. But the Lord blessed them with two daughters, Thalia and Elena. They were bright girls, talented girls. They filled Arzley's and Dagmar's home in Parley Grove with music and with laughter and joy.

The royalties from Arzley's mining interests became substantial during the war. They alone would have provided a comfortable living. But with Dagmar's help, he invested them in commercial real estate—such as there was in Parley Grove. He opened the Parley Grove Western Auto Store. He started up the Lions Club in town. Served two terms as mayor. And he devoted every day of his life to showing Dagmar kindness and making her happy.

Dagmar kept a lovely home. She wore the largest diamond in Parley Grove as modestly as a woman could. She helped Arzley with his books. And she helped him see the goodness all around them through her clearer eyes. And he loved her.

The girls went to college, married well, moved away, and raised fine families.

About ten days ago, Bishop Leland D. Thaxton was visiting Arzley in the care center. The old man was not doing well. Bishop Thaxton held Arzley's hand. They talked about his forty-eight years with Dagmar. Arzley talked about seeing her again, soon, when he could see her without his glasses.

Bishop Thaxton told Arzley he could leave this world a happy man, and proud of his posterity, from those two accomplished daughters, Thalia and Elena.

"Yes sir," Arzley said. "Yes sir. They been good girls. Good girls," he said. "But—and I never said this to anybody before . . . I always thought it was just too bad neither one had a beautiful face like their mother's."

Part of that story's in the hometown weekly, the good news newspaper that helps you remember who you are and where you're from.

LOST SHEEP, PRIZE LAMB

The hometown weekly just came in the mail. The big headline this week:

RECORD BUCK TAKEN IN BOW HUNT

And there's a big picture of LaRoid Haymore showing off his six-point velvet buck with a spread of thirty and a half inches. The story says:

> "This particular animal just might be the third or fourth largest buck taken by bow in the state," said taxidermist DeLeal Lifferth.

Taxidermy is DeLeal's second job. For his day job, he is Parley Grove's veterinarian. The man understands diversification. And with that setup, DeLeal can guarantee you *will* get your dog back—and smiling! Either way!

Well, DeLeal's gonna mount that buck for LaRoid so he can hang it above the TV. And LaRoid's gonna have this whole front page of the weekly laminated, and then he'll slap it on top of the stack of *Field and Stream* down to VarDell's barbershop, just to brag a little.

That's part of what's so wonderful about *The Progress,* and part of what makes it better than television. You can clip it up and save the memories.

Look at this one. I *know* the Ovards have already clipped this out:

Grand Champion Lamb Raised by Parley Grove Girl

First prize at the Taylor County Junior Livestock Show and Auction held last week was won by BreeAnn Ovard for her five-month-old Columbia lamb.

BreeAnn is the ten-year-old daughter of LaMont K. and Marvadel Ovard and the granddaughter of Moylen and Utahna Ovard and Delbert and Marvada Thaxton, all of Parley Grove.

BreeAnn got a lot of money for that lamb—a *lot* of money to a ten-year-old girl. And *The Progress* ran a picture of that curly-haired blond girl and her lamb—just about the cutest pair you ever saw.

The Ovards will save that clipping forever, and they'll never forget that day when BreeAnn sold her lamb . . . her 4-H lamb.

When it came time for the show and the auction, that little girl washed out her lamb's wool with Borax and water and then dried it with towels. She got that wool as white as bleached sheets.

She trimmed it up with a pair of shears and blocked it for hours. She trimmed and polished its hooves and she worked and worked with that lamb so it would stand straight and stand still for the judging.

That lamb was a thing to behold. And BreeAnn did it all by herself. All by herself!

No, the Ovards will never forget that day.

Vern Hundrup won't forget it, either. Although Vern might *like* to forget it. In fact, for a while Vern's been livin' like he would like to forget all about Parley Grove. But he was there that day, and he saw the lamb—saw it *all*, even though he had not even intended to stop in Parley Grove.

Everything was going too well to risk that, with Amber in the seat next to him in the red Ferrari. They were heading north, and she didn't know about the diamond necklace in the glove box. Vern was keeping that a secret until they got to the condo. And Vern figured Parley Grove was not only too far off the main highway, it was *way* too far off message.

But Amber said she'd never been to a real little town. And it didn't make sense to come so far and to be so close to where Vern was from, but not get to see it.

Vern said, "Ah, come on, Babe. There's nothing there to see. Believe me on this one."

Truth was, Vern wasn't sure he could explain Parley Grove to Amber. And he *knew* he couldn't explain Ambrosia to Parley Grove. So right there on the highway, they were having a little disagreement—the first one since Vern had met her at the beach.

Vern *should* have known better, since he was born in Parley Grove forty-one years ago. He was raised there, and he was raised *right,* all the way through the eleventh grade—he and his twin brother. "The Hundrup twins," they called 'em. Then the BLM transferred Meldon, their dad, and they moved up north somewhere. Parley Grove lost track of the Hundrups, seeing's how they weren't natives and had no relatives there and hadn't lived there that long, really—only eighteen years.

Well, time went by, and eventually Vern wound up in Southern California. Which is a long way from Parley Grove, whether you measure in miles or state of mind.

Vern was living in the San Fernando Valley, where he sold cars for DaeWoo Motors of Van Nuys. Life wasn't bad for Vern. He was the top DaeWoo salesman eight years in a row. Had a mortgage on a house on a pretty good street—a three-bedroom stucco house with the attached garage converted to an entertainment room. Had his big-screen digital TV in there, with picture in a picture, so he could watch sixteen shows at the same time. Had a satellite dish on the roof that brought him eight hundred channels. The setup had DVD, laser disk, VCR, MP3, and CD, all with surround sound and with Game Cube and Xbox and Playstation attached. No, life was not bad.

But as Vern got closer to forty, he started feeling restless, as a lot of men unfortunately do at that age, when they realize this is their life and they only get one ride. Vern was in that state of mind, trying to feel young and wild and crazy again, when he paid $135 to go to one of those motivational seminars. It was a real popular seminar, one that's been seen now by nearly 800,000 people—most of *them* pushing forty and wishing they weren't. It was a seminar for people looking for a way out of their frustrations in twelve easy steps—a seminar that promises to change everything in the future while it gives you a little pep talk right now.

The seminar is titled "Unleash the Wild Bull Within." What Vern and about 3,600 other people each paid $135 to see was some guy who flunked out of college wearing a wireless microphone bounding up and down on the stage, whooping and hollering about limitless potential, about power of the possible, and about the supremacy of the self. He explained the negativity that holds underachievers down and the imaginary constraints that stand in the way of you reaching your true self-actualization and your Nirvana and your bliss and your rapture.

He got everybody pretty worked up. Especially Vern. Got 'em all standing and shouting and waving their arms—which was going to help them find their true inspiration . . . their nuclear essence . . . their inner core.

For some people, this stuff really works. Worked for Vern. He discovered right there in that seminar, for $135, that he was not fulfilled. Discovered he wasn't getting all he wanted from life. He decided in that seminar there was *more* out there for him—more than what he already had from putting up with the usual routine. And while Vern stood there, shouting and cheering and waving his arms in the seminar with 3,600 other people, it was just like something inside him snapped. His wild bull, I guess it was. Like it broke its rope. And Vern decided to start over. *His* way.

He quit DaeWoo Motors of Van Nuys and went looking for a rewarding career. Bought a membership at Gold's Gym. Got pretty buff. Leased a Ferrari. Moved out of the house and got an apartment, just for him. Got some new hair—a hair weave—a pretty good one, really. Even got a new name. It was half a name, actually. For all his life he'd been LaVern Hundrup. Now it's just *Vern*. More sophisticated. And I hear his twin brother, who lives in Boise, now just goes by Shirl. So the Hundrup boys aren't LaVern and Shirley any more.

When Vern left the car business, he managed to get in on the ground floor of a fabulous opportunity in multilevel marketing. He became a Triple Platinum-Level distributor for Sea Coast Holistic Supplements, Inc., of Sea Coast, North Dakota. It's a very progressive company. They are the nation's number-one seller of organic kelp capsules. They sell a lot of coastal bee pollen from certified free-range coastal bees. They sell 100 percent natural sea salt, essence of sea spray extract, and rejuvenating sea sand. And their highest-profit margin line is the set of aura-emitting sea shells gathered from pristine shores "after the fair sea creatures have lived out their natural lives to remain forever things of beauty and healing; shells gathered by disadvantaged children in third-world countries who receive a portion of your purchase price, which may enable them to get an education and break out of the cycle of ignorance and poverty." (Actually, they are mostly the children of New Age hippies who live in a commune south of Ensenada.) Sea Coast also sells a lot of fat-free granola and some things like polarity crystals and shoe magnets. And none of the stuff is tested on animals.

Amber found that product line very appealing in a man, as you might expect, since she is pursuing a double major at USC in para-psychic wellness studies and aromatherapy.

Vern met Amber on a Tuesday at Venice Beach. He was rolling down the beach sidewalk showing off his new in-line skates. Amber was on a towel, on the sand, showing off considerably more. Vern stopped and pretended to adjust his skates. She looked up at him and said, "Hi. I'm a Sagittarius!"— which, as Vern thought about it now, was the only time either of them ever mentioned religion.

Vern had never met a girl anything like her—beginning with her tan. Amber had a tan as golden and as deep and as smooth as double-dark creamy peanut butter, which was Vern's favorite comfort food. Just *looking* at her made him hungry. Left him famished. Vern had never seen a tan like that in Parley Grove. People there, if they ever went out in the sun, just turned pink and blotchy, all the way up to their shirt sleeves. Maybe it was something in the water back there. Or something in the diet. Or in the gene pool. Vern wasn't sure. But it was a spectacular tan—looked like an eternal tan, with no beginning and no end, and Amber wore it so well. Which is about all I'd better say about that.

Amber liked Vern's product line from Sea Coast Holistic Supplements, Inc., of Sea Coast, North Dakota, since she is, herself, a vegan. And say what you will about her, the one thing she is absolutely sincere about is not eating meat. As she and Vern got better acquainted, she tried to get him to stop eating animals, too. She said giving up meat would put him in harmony with the life force of the universe. It would add to cosmic peace and congruence. It would help build his aura, bring him good karma, align his ying and his yang. Not to mention what it would do for his hair follicles. And his chronic gas.

It wouldn't be hard, she said, if he'd do it step by step—starting out at first just as a pesco-lacto-ovo vegetarian. Then he could gradually give up fish and then give up milk and then drop eggs. Later, he could give up leather belts and wallets and shoes. Vern proposed dropping all that other stuff first, then gradually tapering off beef, but Amber said that wasn't how it was done. So Vern gave up eating meat when he was with her. The rest of the time he had 'em hold the onions on his Big Macs so she would never know.

Amber was full of ideas that Vern had never heard of. Like aromatherapy—the thought that the right smell could change your whole outlook on life. Ideas that made her seem so exotic. So irresistible. And she *did* smell good. To a man who had not been a drinker, Amber was pure intoxication. And she learned how to play Vern for all he was worth.

This young woman may be a lot of things, but she is not a simple floozy. No, she did not move in with Vern. She stayed with her mother. Her mother is the director of the South Bay Rotweiller Rescue League. That is a nonprofit organization, in the extreme. So Amber *did* let Vern help her with tuition. He had no idea tuition at USC these days was $6,200. A month. And because of the double major in para-psychic wellness studies and aromatherapy, Amber said it would take her about six more years to graduate.

Vern stayed lost in this flirtation for months. He couldn't see how silly she made him look. And he couldn't get the relationship to the next level, despite all the snorting and stamping of his wild bull—which was unleashed and was ferocious, but was just running around in circles. So he decided to up the ante. Vern decided to ask Amber to go with him to his SCHSI convention. He'd get her away from school and away from the beach, where she seemed to spend a lot of her time. For a few heavenly days, he would get her to pay attention to just him, and they might even talk about the future.

Vern had rented a fancy condo in the mountains where they could stay. It had a fireplace. It had a hot tub. He'd be in meetings only a few hours in the mornings, and Amber would look great on his arm at the convention dinners. That diamond necklace in the glove box would give her something to think about. They *looked* like diamonds. If they were cubic zirconium, *I* couldn't tell. And Vern probably knew that Amber couldn't, either. So he asked her if she would drive with him up to Utah.

Amber said she'd never been to Utah. Vern said you could *tell*. It showed. But that would be okay, he said. His convention was in Park City. Park City was different, he said. Park City isn't *really* Utah. Park City is, as Vern explained, the state's *international* zone—a place in Utah where it's okay to be from California. And it is. In fact, you can spend a whole week in Park City and nobody will stare at you for drinking Perrier bottled water—which, as anybody in Parley Grove who's from *real* pioneer stock knows, is an absolutely ridiculous thing to do. Water from the tap is free. And tastes just as good.

In Park City, people eat Asiago and Brie and Provolone. They do not eat Velveeta. When people in Park City dip food in something, they dip it in hummus. They do not dip it in fry sauce. Ask a waiter in Park City for more hummus, and he will say, "My pleasure, sir." He will not say, "You bet." Yes, Park City is different. It's where some Utahns would like to put *all* the people who come from California.

Amber said she would go with him.

So there they were, on the highway, heading north to Park City and passing so close to Parley Grove that Amber said they just had to stop. And she was not taking **no** for an answer. So what was Vern gonna do?

He got off the freeway and followed Highway 89 'til they came to the Parley Grove turnoff. He tried once more to change her mind; he said he had a surprise for her at the condo that would be very special, and he thought they ought to get there before dark. But her mind was made up.

So there they were on the old familiar road leading into his hometown, and after more than twenty years, nothing seemed to have changed. They rounded the turn a mile west of town where the road parallels the irrigation canal and the poplar trees; they drove in past the feed store next to the old county fair barn. They saw the barn was surrounded by about a hundred pickup trucks, as well as a few cars, parked there in the field.

Amber wanted to know, "What's that all about?"

Vern said this time of year, on a Saturday, it would probably be the 4-H auction.

"I want to see it," Amber said.

Vern said, "Ah, you're a city girl. You don't want to see that!"

"Don't you tell me what I do and don't want to see, Vern Hundrup. If you expect a good time, you'd better start taking me seriously. *Now!*"

This came as a surprise to Vern. But she had him. She had him good. And he did not have a positive feeling about the way this would turn out.

They walked inside the old show arena. Vern's Armani sunglasses made it hard to see, but he wasn't going to take them off. Or the Dodgers cap, either. He hoped that with that much of a disguise and twenty-four years, nobody would recognize him. But the two of them stuck out in that crowd like antlers on a duck! Vern was the only man in the place not in Wranglers and boots. And Amber was the only woman in hot pants. She found a spot in the bleachers, and Vern had to follow.

The auction was underway, with Varlo Belcher playing auctioneer like he's done forever. He's not that good at it, but he's all they've got. Little BreeAnn Ovard with her curly blond hair was standing in the ring next to her grand champion lamb, and Varlo opened the bidding at $50.

It went to $55. Then $60. Then $65. Amber asked Vern what this was all about. He told her how kids raise the animals, bring 'em there to be judged, and then the best ones go up for auction.

"Who buys them?" Amber asked.

"Anybody," Vern said. "A few boosters and relatives usually jack up the price a little to make the kids feel good—even if they lose a few bucks on the resale to the packing plant."

Amber gasped. "Packing plant?! *Meat* packing plant?!"

Then she stood up and shouted, "One hundred dollars!"

Varlo said, "One hundred dollars to the—lady! Now $110, asking $110."

Vern said, "What do you think you're *doing?*"

"What do you *mean?*" Amber said. "Give me your wallet!"

Delbert Thaxton, BreeAnn's grandpa, eyed these out-of-towners. He didn't know who they were, but he wasn't going to let them cut in on his special deal.

"One hundred twenty-five!" Delbert said.

BreeAnn looked at her Grandpa Thaxton, and a tear rolled down her cheek.

Amber said, "Oh, Vern. That little girl is starting to cry. They're going to take away her little lamb and send it to the meat packing plant. This is awful."

At that point, Grandpa Ovard joined the bidding to give Delbert Thaxton a little fun. "One hundred thirty-five," Grandpa Ovard said.

The bids were going up fast, and BreeAnn's eyes filled with tears. Amber pulled Vern's wallet from his hand as Delbert said, "One hundred fifty."

Amber shouted, "Two hundred!"

Vern said, "Are you crazy?"

She flashed him a look he'd never seen from her before—a look that was sharp and loathing.

BreeAnn was crying now. She was bawling, shaking, holding her face in her hands.

Amber did a quick count of the bills in Vern's plastic wallet, then shouted, **"Five hundred eighty-six dollars!"**

The place got quiet except for BreeAnn's sobbing.

Vern said, "Are you *nuts?*"

She repeated, "Five hundred eighty-six dollars for the lamby!" and she waved the bills at the auctioneer.

You could have heard a pin drop.

Finally, Varlo said, "Sold, for $586 to the lady from—from—not around here."

The little girl shrieked.

Amber jumped down from the bleachers, ran to the ring, and threw her arms around the child.

"It's okay, Baby. It's okay," she said. "I know how you feel. But it's all right. Because here's the money. This is your money, Baby. And I want you to keep your little lamby."

This time BreeAnn's scream was over the top—one of those screams only a ten-year-old girl knows how to scream. Amber let her go, took two steps back, then held the child's face in her hands.

"I said you can keep the money, and your lamby, too. What part don't you understand? Why are you still crying?"

BreeAnn wiped her eyes with her arm. She said, "I've been crying, cause I can't believe, like, how much I'm gonna get for this—stupid sheep! I thought, like, I'd be lucky to get, like, a hundred bucks. But, like, five hundred and how many? For *Butthead?* Oh, my heck! This is so, like, *awesome!*"

People close enough to hear the conversation started to chuckle. Their faces told Amber that she was standing on foreign soil, and she did not speak the local language.

Vern came up from behind and pulled on her arm. "It's time to get out of here," he said. "If you're coming with me, we're leaving now."

The Ovards were loading Butthead back into the truck when Grandpa Thaxton said to Grandpa Ovard, "Well, Moylen, feels to me like we give them slickers the real Bible treatment."

"How's that?" Moylen asked.

"Well, sure seems like in Matthew, they was strangers, and we took 'em."

I wish I knew the rest of the story—what those two people from California said to each other after they got back in that red car. I wish I knew which way they turned when they got back to the main highway and what happened after *that.* It would be interesting to know.

I do know the Ovards are still pretty happy.

BreeAnn's got a blue ribbon on her wall, this clipping from the weekly in her scrapbook, and $500 in the bank.

And there's lamb chops in the freezer.

So it's all good. *All good* news.

And *part* of that story's in the hometown weekly, the good news newspaper that helps you remember who you are and where you're from.

THE
PARLEY'S PROGRESS
SERVING PARLEY GROVE, UTAH'S 87TH LARGEST CITY, AND ALL OF TAYLOR COUNTY

THE PUMPKIN AND THE PILLOWCASE

The hometown weekly just came in the mail. There are a couple of good press releases masquerading as news stories this week under the headlines:

MORE CALCIUM, FEWER HIP FRACTURES

and

CANKER SORES BEST TREATED BY DOCTOR OR DENTIST

Things seem pretty calm these days in Parley Grove. The lead headline this week:

MEETING HELD BY PG CITY COUNCIL

This month, like most, there's not much news from the council minutes. The story says:

> **Presiding was mayor Naff Dilson.**
> **Also in attendance were city council members Vee Orth, Bridger Turpin,**

Dionna Thorkelson, and Delwood
Pollard. Councilman LeNard Blatter
was absent.

Presented to the council was
Ammon Dorton's proposed Eagle Scout
project to collect used books for the
city library. Ammon was commended
by the council for his plans.

Discussed was a citizen proposal
from Caprice Drabner for an ordinance
regulating the storage of old vehicles.
No action was taken.

If you've seen councilman Vee Orth's front yard, you know that no such
ordinance will ever get past *him*. Caprice lives across the street from Vee,
and, as you might have guessed, she's not from around here. In fact, she came
from California, where people have different ideas about government, and
where some believe in socialism.

None of that's too newsy, but it's all good news, as far as it goes. At least
the government won't be telling Vee Orth what he can and can't do with his
own trucks on his own property.

Not that Vee isn't civic-minded. Because he is. In fact, Vee has taken it
upon himself as a city council member to spearhead economic development
proposals for Parley Grove. He understands the need for Parley Grove to create a
unique identity—something to make it stand out from all the other nondescript,
struggling little towns up and down the middle of the state and, for that matter,
all the thousands of struggling little towns from sea to shining sea.

Vee has told 'em, "It's a world market these days. This is the age of
globalization, and you have got to adapt. At the end of the day, it's not the
town's size," he tells the council, "or even the town's *location*"—which is good
news, since they can't do a thing about *that*—"it's the town's *image*." Vee
says perception is everything in the business of promotion. And Vee tells
'em, "Parley Grove needs to present to potential industry and tourists and
developers some value-added identity." And they listen.

Vee's proposals have been evolving. One of the ideas he started out
with, after considering what the town *has,* was to promote Parley Grove as
the home of the world's largest ball of used baling wire. Thurman Fackler
has been working on that ball for nearly forty years, ever since they started

phasing out baling wire in favor of baling twine. But twine, you see, is not as durable or nearly as useful as wire. Thurman saw that from the start.

Twine may be easier on the hands when you pitch the bales, and easier to snip, and easier on a cow if she swallows a piece of it. But you can't mend fences with twine, and you can't use twine in place of a tailgate hinge, and twine's worth nothin' as a mount for your muffler. Twine's no good as an antenna or for any electrical work at all, and it's useless on a cracked shovel handle. No, sometimes progress takes you backwards. And without baling wire, people nowadays try to get by with nothing more than Superglue and duct tape.

So long about the late 1960s, Thurman—who always saved baling wire anyway, and who, as a prudent man from pioneer stock, *will* use it up and wear it out, make it do or do without (which *is* the *Ode to Baling Wire*)—started hoarding baling wire as farmers were converting over to twine. Thurman also has a network of suppliers who find used baling wire in old barns around the country and who send it to him. He even buys some of it on eBay. He's been winding it tightly into a ball for more than thirty years. It's now twenty-eight feet in diameter and has just about outgrown his old hay barn. Thurman hasn't had hay in there since '96, when he sold his last cows.

Now *there's* a resource Vee told 'em could set Parley Grove apart: give it identity as the home of the world's largest ball of used baling wire. You could sell postcards with pictures of the ball and key chains with the ball on them—maybe even key chains made *from* it. You could make mugs and T-shirts and hats with pictures of the world's largest ball of used baling wire on 'em. That might lead to promotional slogans like, "Parley Grove, Wired for Business" or "Parley Grove, Wired for Size" or just "Parley Grove, Home of the World's Largest Ball of Used Baling Wire."

The council thought they might have something there, until Dionna Thorkelson Googled *baling wire, ball, world's largest,* and found a website for a ball of baling wire in Manitoba that's thirty-two feet in diameter—four feet bigger than Thurman's ball. And at the bottom of the page was a link to a website for a ball of used baling wire in Wisconsin that's thirty-one feet in diameter. That sort of took the wind out of their sails, because they knew "World's *Third*-Largest Ball of Used Baling Wire" just wouldn't cut it as the foundation for economic development. People are just funny that way. It's too bad, but if it's not *the* biggest, they're not impressed. It's too bad people won't recognize achievement for what it is, instead of always comparing everything. Because Thurman has done a commendable job.

For a while Vee was pushing a North American mule deer trophy museum. Parley Grove *is* mule deer country. And there is no such museum to display all the record racks. Vee said, "Think of all the hunters who would come to see that." Well, they did think about it. And they did some research, and found that deer hunting is a declining sport—not in Parley Grove, of course, but around the country, fewer and fewer people go deer hunting each year. So the council decided they needed to come up with something that would tie into a growth industry, not a declining industry.

Vee's been thinking about that for a while, and last month he proposed that Parley Grove offer incentives for the establishment of the MLM hall of fame. What Cooperstown is to baseball, he said, Parley Grove could be to multilevel marketing. Which is entirely appropriate, since multilevel marketing was *invented* in Parley Grove—which is a story for another time. And with a proprietary database, the MLM hall of fame could gather all the information to recognize and honor all the top distributors of Amway and Mary Kay and Herbalife and Pampered Chef and *their* people, and the up-and-coming distributors and *their* people and the latest distributors of all the MLM companies.

Vee could see this multilevel marketing hall of fame drawing all the people in the world who've ever sold Sunrider or NuSkin or Nature's Sunshine or Omegatrend. They would come to have the interactive experience with a touch-screen database containing all the top performers of all the MLM companies worldwide. (There *is,* undeniably, a real draw to seeing your name on a screen.) And they could advertise it on the World Wide Web as the one place in the world where people could access that database of multilevel marketing champions—and that one place would be in Parley Grove!

"And," Vee said, "think how many folks would come to see *that! These* are people who get motivated by lapel pins!"

They might even have displays and dioramas—maybe even a water ride—that would take you through the history of multilevel marketing with animation and sound effects. It could be kind of like a multilevel marketing "Pirates of the Caribbean."

So this is the latest economic development proposal still under advisement by the Parley Grove town council.

And here's what EvaDean Thiede says this week:

OUT 'N ABOUT
By EvaDean Thiede

**The frost is on the pumpkins, and
the cornstalks all are brown. By the**

time you read this, both the hunt and Halloween will be behind us, and the deer can let down their guard.

Among those visiting last month for the hunt were Kayden Thaxton and his family from Alpine. Kayden is the son of Garlan and Arthella Thaxton and the brother of Bishop Leland D. Thaxton, all of Parley Grove. Kayden not only won the rifle at the Deer Hunters Ball, but Arthella says he also got a six-point buck with a twenty-eight-inch rack.

Quite frankly, that was all just about more than Bishop Thaxton—beloved man that he is—could endure from his little brother. People don't give bishops credit for having struggles like the rest of us have. But bishops have issues in their families, too: sibling rivalries, disappointments, second thoughts. That doesn't all go away just because you wear the mantle. And Kayden's visit, and Kayden's deer, and Kayden's overwhelming worldly success were all pretty hard on Bishop Thaxton last month.

The bishop was ever the dutiful son—the one who returned to his roots after going to college, and then, coming home to look after his folks, he found the peak of his career achievement (so far) as the shop teacher at Parley Grove High. He also teaches two classes of freshman English, and he farms a little acreage on the side.

His brother Kayden—his *younger* brother—dropped out of college. But he got all the recognition and success. He is now director of merchandising for Fijian Bula Nutrition International, with its bula jams and bula jellies from the fruit of the Fijian bula plant, and bula extract that you drink straight from the bottle—if you're *man* enough. And if you do drink it, you *will* be a man. Or you can take the pills or the concentrate or the wafers, laced with what for thousands of years the islanders have called "the mother of all medicines." A lot of people believe it makes them feel better. Kayden knows it makes *him* filthy rich.

It was not a good start for Bishop Thaxton when Kayden pulled up to the homestead driving his new Lexus SUV. The bishop drives an old Ford Ranger. It was not a great start, and it went mostly south from there, long before they and their dad and the boys ever got on the mountain. Kayden came outfitted in some fancy new get-up from REI. It was a lightweight, water-wicking, thermal-insulated, poly-hypoallergenic, perma-pressed, modular, outdoor survival *system*. He brought a GPS with a built-in altimeter and emergency locator transmitter, a rifle with a scope that you look through and can see the moons of Jupiter, a set of satellite-relayed walkie-talkies, and a battery-powered electric sleeping bag. And then he had the nerve to say how nice it was to be home again, where people are close to nature.

Kayden told the bishop he really ought to let Kayden set him up as a Fijian Bula Nutrition distributor. Kayden said if the bishop worked at it, even part time, he could probably clear forty grand the first year, even from a little town like this. He could recruit his next level of salespeople anywhere. He must know some people in real cities, Kayden said. And being the bishop, Kayden told him, wouldn't hurt him with sales in Parley Grove.

He said, "If you clear $50K by the end of next year, you could qualify for the trip to Aruba. Defra would probably like that. I don't think you guys have been anywhere since you got married, have you?"

He said, "You ought to think about it. So many people are stuck in the mindset their whole lives of trying to work harder, and they never get ahead. The secret is to work *smarter*. You just have to decide if you have it in you."

And the more Bishop Thaxton thought about it, the more he decided he did not.

I wouldn't say that what the bishop was feeling was envy. He was not breaking the tenth commandment that says not to covet. Not technically. But by the time he finally bagged his scrawny little two-point buck, long after Kayden had dressed out his *lord of the forest*, Bishop Leland D. Thaxton *was* feeling a little self-pity. And it stayed with him. It stayed with him clear through Halloween.

On Halloween he took his little boy, Kodi, through the neighborhood to trick-or-treat for the first time. Kodiak is three. Defra had bought him a *Finding Nemo* costume up at the WalMart in Richfield. Dressed him up like a fish. The kid was so cute.

Clear back in September, the Thaxtons started building Halloween up for Kodi—telling him how much fun Halloween was going to be. They talked about how he'd go door-to-door with his dad, and how he'd say "trick-or-treat," and make a noise like a fish, and how people would give him candy. He was all excited about that wonderful night. (Just like some of you get. And you *know* who you are.)

Little Kodi could not wait! On October 28, he got up at four in the morning, came into his parents' room in his Nemo costume, and asked, "Is it Halloween today?"

When the big night finally came, Defra put him in a sweater, put him in a pair of warm overalls, put his Nemo costume on over the top, and gave him the little plastic pumpkin she splurged on at WalMart—the plastic pumpkin that would hold his loot.

They took a picture of him, all dressed up. And then Kodi headed out with his dad.

At every house they went to, Bishop Thaxton lifted him up to help him ring the bell or knock on the door. And then the bishop stepped back toward the road and stood in the shadows while his little boy shouted "Trick-or-treat!" and made his noise like a fish. He jumped up and down every time somebody gave him one more piece of candy, and he waved to his dad, the bishop, who was standing back out there on the road, still feeling kind of sorry for himself.

Well, after they went up one side of his street and back down the other, this little kid was overjoyed. Halloween had been everything Kodiak had hoped for, and now he was getting kind of cold and a little bit tired. It was nearly seven o'clock, and he was ready to call it a night.

Back home, the girls were still gone, making their rounds. Defra didn't know where Cougar was. So Kodi had center stage. He dumped the treats from his plastic pumpkin onto the floor in the living room. Such a pile they made! He started sorting the pieces—grouped them by kind (just like some of you do—and you *know* who you are).

He had:

3 Tootsie Rolls

2 Tootsie Pops

1 Twix

2 Milk Duds

1 Snickers bar—full size!

4 Starbursts

2 fun-size Three Musketeers

3 fun-size Hershey bars

1 Kit Kat

2 Hot Tamales boxes

1 candy cane from the Windborgs (which was left over from last Christmas)

2 Reese's Pieces

1 little package of Whoppers

1 roll of Smarties (which contains nineteen individual pieces)

1 Sugar Daddy

1 homemade cookie wrapped in a plastic baggie from Sister Belcher, who doesn't know you're not supposed to fix homemade stuff any more because it might have razor blades in it

And he had a toothbrush from Brother Skog, who is the dentist and who has no sense of humor.

Kodi counted up the total: twenty-seven packages of candy! Plus the toothbrush and the cookie (that probably had a razor blade in it).

Twenty-seven pieces of candy!

It was the best night of his life! Kodie was so happy that it even cheered up the bishop, just a little.

About then, the older (much older—nearly seventeen) Thaxton boy, Cougar, came home. He and some other guys had decided on the spur of the moment that they'd go trick-or-treating, too. There's no definite cut-off age for it. And they figure you've got to have fun while you can.

Cougar didn't have a costume. He just went down to the basement and found an old mask—a Richard Nixon mask. That was *it*. He just wore that mask and his sweats.

A couple of the other guys put green paint on their faces. One of them pulled a nylon stocking over his head. That *can* make you look horrible, but on Travis, it might have been an improvement.

The last guy wore just a ponytail he found in his sister's bedroom.

They worked on their costumes for all of five minutes total, and Cougar grabbed the pillowcase off his bed to use for a sack.

So while little Kodi was home counting and sorting his twenty-seven wonderful pieces of candy, these five big guys were out pillaging all of Parley Grove.

They ran from house to house, looking like they were heeding the counsel to put away a year's supply.

Truth be told, some people don't really like it when kids that big come trick-or-treating.

But when you answer the door and see two mean green faces, a guy with his head in pantyhose, some dude with a blond ponytail, and Richard Nixon, all on your front porch, you just hand 'em the candy real quick and hope they'll go away.

After a couple of hours of that, they'd done the whole town, and Cougar came home with the pillowcase over his shoulder. It must have weighed twelve or thirteen pounds. It was disgusting.

He dumped the massive haul from his pillowcase next to the pieces his little brother had collected in the plastic pumpkin.

Kodi had been asleep on the floor, but the noise woke him up. And he looked at the huge pile of candy that wasn't *his*, but was his *brother's*. And he looked back at his twenty-seven little pieces—actually down to twenty-two by then—and he looked back at the big pile, and then back at the little pile, and then back at the big pile, and then he started to cry. All the joy he'd been feeling for a month drained right out of him. The little boy ran to his daddy and cried in his arms. He cried over the disappointment of Halloween.

Cougar looked up and said, "What's the deal with *him?*"

"Well," his dad said, "how would *you* like it if somebody came along and made everything you thought was wonderful look like nothin'?"

The teenager said, "That's stupid, Dad! You got to explain it to him."

The bishop said, "Explain what?"

"Well, shoot," Cougar said. "He's gotta know life *don't* have to be *perfect*."

"*Doesn't*," his dad said. "'*Doesn't* have to be' . . . not '*Don't* have to be.'"

"Sheeze! *Whatever!*" Cougar said as he poured a box of Milk Duds down his throat.

Bishop Thaxton rocked little Kodi back to sleep while he stewed over his older boy's grammar. He also stewed about what Cougar had *said:* "Life don't have to be *perfect.*" And he thought about it some more. And he thought about his life.

He thought about that little boy in his arms in the fish costume, and about all four of his kids, and about Defra. He thought about the good people in the ward and all the other good folks in Parley Grove. And then he thought about that moment on the morning of the hunt last week, just as the sun crept up over Mount Baldy and shot its sharp spikes through the sky and filled the whole world with brightness. That had been some moment.

And the more he thought about it all, the more he felt that *his* life was . . . really not so bad, even with a brother like Kayden.

The parable of the pumpkin and the pillowcase made for a nice message from the pulpit on Fast Sunday. So Bishop Thaxton carries on. And he's cheered up. And *you* probably should cheer up, too. Because his boy was right, you know. It is true: Life *don't* have to be *perfect* to be pretty darn *good.*

Part of that story's in the hometown weekly, the good news newspaper that helps you remember who you are and where you're from.

HANGING BY A THREAD

The hometown weekly just came in the mail. On the front page are the results of the general election a week ago Tuesday. The chart shows you not just who won, since *that* was hardly in doubt, but also how many votes each candidate got in the county, *by precinct;* and how many voters are registered in each precinct; and how many of the voters in each precinct actually voted. That was the *real* suspense, because the only race on the whole ballot with more than one candidate was the one for Congress—which, of course, involved more than Taylor County.

And like Norbert said, "After all, this district now takes in part of Salt Lake City, for heck's sakes!" That's what Norbert Egbert said to the men down to VarDell's Barbershop on Thursday afternoon. That was after the returns were in, and they showed that the voters in the district had elected the *wrong man* to Congress.

Norbert said, "There's *some* people up to Salt Lake these days who got no more sense than God give a crowbar."

Just about everybody chimed in with "Ain't *that* the truth" or "Darn right!" Except for Brother Rasmussen. He was trying to quote the scripture that says it isn't common that the greater part of the people should desire the wrong thing.

"But it just goes to show," Brother Rasmussen said, "we are living in perilous times." And all the rest of 'em pretty much agreed with that, too. But then VarDell pointed out that the mistake for Congress wasn't Taylor County's doing. It wasn't *their* fault. They took *some* comfort in that. And VarDell said that Taylor County could be proud that it had one of the highest voter turnouts in the state.

VarDell's job is to administer the haircuts—or, we should say, the hair*cut*. It's pretty much a one-size-fits-all proposition at VarDell's. It's his job to administer the cut and to lead the conversation, if it lags. Of course, he knows to stay away from controversy, so he steers the talk toward *safe* subjects, like politics and religion and guns and huntin'—the things people all agree on. He knows *not* to let 'em get into dangerous territory—like Ford trucks versus Chevrolets—or other things that could lead to fist fights.

They agreed that the turnout might have been even higher than usual this year. Taylor County voters are dedicated supporters of the electoral process, even when there's only one slate of candidates. Maybe *especially* when there's only one slate of candidates. Because that way they are sure the people they vote for—the *right* people—are the people who are gonna win.

And except for that mess for Congress (which *wasn't* Taylor County's fault), they nearly had a perfect ballot this year: one candidate for every office. That keeps politics orderly—or, as Brother Rasmussen saw it, "without dissension," he said, "or confusion, or evil speaking, or hard-heartedness, or the spirit of contention," which he reminded 'em all comes of the devil. The county elections were fine, *except* for county surveyor, which was a huge embarrassment to just about everybody and a particular sadness to Brother Rasmussen.

There had been talk by the commission of doing away with county surveyor—it *is* only a part-time job—and just hiring out what survey work there is. And that's what they were going to do last year when Belwin Norby said he was retiring, because he *is* seventy-eight years old. Belwin has been county surveyor for thirty-six years, nearly half his life. But the thought of doing away with the office was a great blow to hometown pride. It was especially a blow to the sensibilities of Brother Rasmussen. It cut him to the heart just to think of the shrinking of democracy, when democracy *is,* of course, an expression of agency, which *is* a heavenly gift.

Brother Rasmussen received his call early to uphold democracy and freedom. And since it's a call, he keeps his exhortations positive—uses *positive* words—and doesn't stoop to name-calling. Brother Rasmussen *knows* there must be opposition in all things, and even offenses. That's just the way it is. But as he always says, "Woe unto them by whom it comes." So he is very civil, unlike some of the others down to VarDell's, who just call 'em as they see 'em when they talk about the other side. They just flat out call 'em "liberal, commie-pinko, dope-smokin', tree-hugging, hippy environmentalists."

Now, Brother Rasmussen *never* says things like that. It would be beneath his dignity, which is *considerable,* and beneath the stature he has assumed.

I suspect the source of that stature is related to his having been called *Brother Rasmussen* for so long—in fact, for all his sixty-seven years. Being called by a name like that from the time he was a kid has set Brother Rasmussen apart from all the Delmos and the Thurlows and the Norberts down to VarDell's and everywhere else in Parley Grove. "Brother Rasmussen" just sounds more worthy than "Buck" or "Gloyd" or "LaVorn" or "Dunk." It's been a heavy burden for him to carry, I suppose, but that's the burden he's had to live with. Because that's what his mother named him!

Actually, his mother chose the name *Broder,* which is a good Danish name. It means "brother," but it's a first name in Danish. He could have gotten off easy with *that,* but old Dr. Prisbee had had enough of those Scandinavian names. After three generations he thought it was time they got with the program—so on the birth certificate, he wrote it in English: *Brother.* And it stuck.

Brother Rasmussen has tried to live up to his name. And he's done a pretty good job, both on the church side and on the civic side—which have always been pretty much the same side to him, since a double-minded man is unstable in all his ways, as it says in the Book of Proverbs, and as he will tell you. That name made Brother a pious child. And he was a straight-arrow teen back in the fifties when he won the Parley Grove Fourth of July speech contest. He delivered his speech from a pulpit up on a flatbed trailer, parked behind the school in the shade. It was a powerful oration, entitled "Defenders of Our Freedom: Washington, Lincoln, and Senator Joseph McCarthy." Young Brother Rasmussen built that speech up to a mighty crescendo, right to where he ended it with "Amen." The crowd wasn't sure what the protocol was with a thing like that, so first they said "Amen," and *then* they clapped, and *then* they clapped and stood! It was a defining moment for a teenage boy.

So Brother Rasmussen found his calling early, and this year he sorrowed at the thought of losing the freely elected office of county surveyor. But the practical consideration was that nobody else in Taylor County had a surveyor's license.

Until Ethan Fitzpatrick moved in.

He's a nice young fellow, Ethan is, but he's not from around *here*—not from around Parley Grove at all—and Brother Rasmussen used to remind 'em all at VarDell's how important it is to know a man's background and his people and who they are and where they're from. And then he got real quiet, Brother Rasmussen did, and he looked up at the ceiling, and water filled his eyes, and he confessed to 'em all with a tremor in his voice that he himself had failed to know all there was to know about this Ethan Fitzpatrick, and he had nearly led the people astray. He said, "I pray you will forgive me." Then he cleared his throat and blew his sizable nose into his handkerchief to underline what he'd said. It got real quiet in the barbershop—so quiet it was almost *reverent*—until VarDell turned his clippers back on. Brother Rasmussen cleared his throat again and wiped his eyes.

Ethan Fitzpatrick was going to college in Ohio when he joined the Mormon Church and transferred to the BYU. He'd been in civil engineering before, which was how he picked up surveying. But in Provo he decided it was his calling in life to be a seminary teacher—to bring up teenagers in the faith. Trouble was, landing that job was a struggle with his short resume. Then he met and married Feldon Soderstrom's youngest daughter, Laycee, who was up in Provo. And when Ethan graduated last year, they moved to Parley Grove, mostly to have a place to live for a while with Laycee's parents (Feldon and VerJean), but also to help Feldon out on his place, since his arthritis has been slowing him down.

The Soderstroms weren't sure about Ethan at first, but Feldon says the boy's a real good worker for being a city kid and being from the East, and being a *convert* and all. But he hasn't been able to pay him much. So it was a godsend in January when Ethan got hired part-time to teach two classes a day at the Mormon seminary next to Parley Grove High School.

And he's been a popular teacher. Lots of energy. Lots of pizazz. For a lesson on Daniel, he went down to DeLeal's taxidermy place, and he talked DeLeal into lending him some props—the closest things he had to lions for a lion's den, which turned out to be two stuffed cougars and a bobcat. And DeLeal threw in a rattlesnake for good measure. Ethan sneaked them into the seminary building and set them up in the front of the classroom. Then he strung a clothesline across the room and hung sheets over it so you couldn't see what was hiding behind the sheets. And he put that coiled rattlesnake on his desk, just about at eye level to the kids.

Well, the next morning, first period, after the devotional, Ethan—that is, *Brother Fitzpatrick* to the kids—said he had a story from the Bible "of a young person much like you. A person who came to find the true source of his strength." And he had them turn to Daniel 6.

Ethan told the story of Daniel—who, by the strength of his conviction and the steadfastness of his faith, rose to become the right-hand man to the king of Babylon. But then he told how Daniel's enemies hatched a plot and got him thrown into a den of lions, just for being good. And how they sealed the den with a great stone that made it dark—"pitch dark," Ethan said, as he turned out the lights. He said, "Close your eyes and imagine how dark it was down there in the lions' den through the night. Imagine the growls and the roars Daniel heard. Imagine *you* are Daniel. Keep your eyes closed, and imagine. How hard would you pray?"

Ethan is good at theater, and the kids were starting to get into this. Ethan played up how the lions would brush up against you in the dark and make you wonder where they were gonna bite you first. He had their attention, imagining this kind of thing going on all night long. Then in the morning, he told them, the king came and removed the stone. "And for the first time you can see!" he cried. He cut the clothesline and turned on the lights as he said, "Open your eyes!"

Well, there on the front row, middle seat, Brittani Seegmiller opened her eyes just inches from the eyes of that rattlesnake. Brittani *screamed!* Then *all* the girls screamed. Brittani jumped up on her chair—and then she saw the cougars and the bobcat staring at her, and she screamed again. Then **everybody** was screaming. Finally, some of the boys started to laugh, and Brittani jumped off her chair and screamed again and ran out the door— because, as she explained later, "Oh my gosh, 'fer rills, I just, like, totally *freaked!*"

So much adrenalin in that room! Ethan had those kids wound tighter than twine on a hay baler! Talk about feeling the Spirit! It was the most wonderful thing that ever *happened* in seminary!

Word about this got around so fast that all the other kids were trying to change their schedules so they could get out of Brother Eckberg's classes and get into one of Brother Fitzpatrick's classes.

Ethan was finally feeling useful. He was feeling fulfilled. The next week, he brought in his surveyor's equipment, his transit and his tripod and his plumb bob and his steel tape—props for a wonderful lesson about charting your way and walking the straight and narrow path. And *that's* how word got out that he was a licensed surveyor.

That stuff was still in the classroom when Brother Rasmussen went up to the seminary to meet with him, as soon as he heard, to feel him out and see if he would be "qualified."

Brother Rasmussen asked Ethan how he liked his part-time job teaching seminary. Ethan said he loved it, and he loved the kids. Brother Rasmussen said, "Well, Brother Fitzpatrick, I'm sure you love the Lord, too." And Ethan said of course he did.

"And do you love this nation?" Brother Rasmussen asked that with a tremor in his voice.

Ethan said of course he did.

Brother Rasmussen said, "Yes, it is choice above all other lands."

Then Brother Rasmussen looked at the transit on the tripod and asked Ethan what he did with that. Ethan said he used it as a tool in surveying to chart straight—not crooked—lines. Brother Rasmussen liked that a lot. He asked Ethan if he believed in Constitutional principles. Ethan said he did. He asked if Ethan supported or agreed with any positions of the Council on Foreign Relations or the Trilateralists. Ethan said that he did not, so far as he knew. Brother Rasmussen asked if he advocated fluoride in Parley Grove's drinking water. Ethan swore he'd never given that any thought.

Ethan passed those questions well enough, so Brother Rasmussen got down to the real business. He took out his handkerchief, which is always a signal from Brother Rasmussen that something's *coming*. He cleared his throat, he looked up at the ceiling, and water filled his eyes. Then he fixed those eyes firmly on Ethan and asked him to ponder and pray over the possibility of running for Taylor County surveyor. Because, if it was right for him to do, Brother Rasmussen said he would tell the county commission, and they would not abolish the office. They would hold it open for his election. It was part-time, flexible hours. And it paid $890 a month.

Well, Ethan felt like the hand of Providence had just patted him on the back. His prayers had been answered. Teaching seminary and surveying, too, just when he and Laycee'd learned they had a baby on the way.

Ethan promised to file with the county clerk's office before the deadline, and the commission included county surveyor in the official posting of positions open this year. *That* made a headline in the weekly on the first of March:

ELECTED SURVEYOR POST TO BE KEPT, COMMISSION DECIDES

So it was on the record and couldn't be changed, which is what led to this embarrassment, this civic crisis, and this blotch on Brother Rasmussen's good name.

There in VarDell's barbershop on Thursday, Brother Rasmussen dabbed his eyes with his handkerchief. He wasn't there for a haircut as much as for an audience. He dabbed his eyes with his handkerchief and led the men through the election results as printed in the weekly, one more time.

He began with State Representative LaFaun Pollard, who had run unopposed. Which was as it should be, Brother Rasmussen reminded them, because LaFaun "espouses correct principles and always votes the way he *should*. Never voted for a tax increase on anything. He *deserved* a sixth term."

Likewise, Heston Newbold will stay Commission chairman for four more years, defending against the onslaught of anarchy and tyranny and communism. Brother Rasmussen said, "He's very knowledgeable about those things."

That brought 'em to Commission Seat B. It was open, since Nylan Hooley was retiring. But Monalaine Pasket stepped in to carry on. Actually,

Brother Rasmussen had recruited her, too. He told the men, "Sister Pasket can recite the entire Bill of Rights by heart, all ten amendments."

Next was Oreta Horsley, who was reelected. She ran on the promise that the office of county clerk/auditor would continue to stand firm against the pernicious evil of socialized medicine.

Treasurer LaZell Yotter had renewed his pledge to defend against the international bankers and their secret conspiracies, and the treasons of the UN, and the lies of the Sierra Club. And the way Brother Rasmussen told it, they could *all* be massing their forces together for attack any day, just over the county line.

Then Brother Rasmussen said, "And county assessor." His voice trembled again. "Never a question there."

Everybody agreed with Brother Rasmussen on that. The whole stake votes for President RDell C. Markum every year in conference. President Markum doesn't play that up. He just ran again unopposed, on a record of competence.

Next on the list came county attorney. To run for that office you have to *be* an attorney. So in Taylor County, Narlan Minroy has a lock on the job.

Brother Rasmussen continued his recitation of the elected and the elect. He moved on to Sheriff Buck Heckman, who will keep on keeping the peace. He's a straight law-and-order man who heads a loyal force of three.

So Taylor County is in good hands. And it was a tidy election. Except for surveyor, which Brother Rasmussen confessed between sniffles, was the biggest public shame in Taylor County ever since DewEtta Fackler—who was a notary public and a widow—took up with that Catholic man from Louisiana and left town.

"But," Brother Rasmussen said, "the Lord sendeth rain on the just and the unjust." And he put his handkerchief back in his pocket.

Well, Ethan Fitzpatrick may be a licensed surveyor. And the kids in seminary said he *was* a good teacher. But the guy didn't know the first thing about politics, not in Parley Grove. And how he could have done what he did is beyond me. You see, when Ethan made it to the courthouse last March to file for surveyor, it was just before five o'clock on the final day. He paid his filing fee, and he filled out the form, and he checked the box to run—now *this* could offend some people, I know, and I'm *sorry*—to run as a **Democrat!**

Of course, Oreta Horsley—the county clerk/auditor—caught the mistake and said she'd get some Whiteout so Ethan could fix it.

"Not a mistake," Ethan said. All of his family are Democrats, for five generations. That's what Fitzpatricks are.

Oreta caught her breath, and she turned pale. She *runs* the county elections, and this would be a blemish on *her* record. She called Brother Rasmussen on the phone.

That evening Brother Rasmussen found Ethan up to the seminary, working on his next lesson—a lesson about Jonah. He'd set up a twenty-five-gallon aquarium on his desk, with a four-pound brown trout he got from the hatchery. And he had little crackers—they were like animal crackers in the shape of men—that he would drop in there for the fish to swallow. And he was practicing to make sure it would swallow 'em whole, because he wanted the kids to be thinking about Jonah, not about *Jaws*.

The door was open. Brother Rasmussen gave a little knock. Ethan looked up. He said, "Hey, Brother Rasmussen. Come in."

Brother Rasmussen stepped inside and took out the handkerchief.

He sniffled. He looked at the ceiling. He drew a breath and, on cue, water filled his eyes. Brother Rasmussen cleared his throat, and then from down inside that throat came a cry, a wail straight from the Book of Lamentations. There were words of woe and grief and pain, and that thing in his throat caught at all the right places. It was a fantastic performance! And Ethan didn't have a *clue* what he was talking about.

Brother Rasmussen took a deep breath and blew his nose and wiped it twice, and he looked Ethan in the eye. He said, "Brother Fitzpatrick, we send our children to you because we trusted you." He wiped his eyes. He said, "Brother Fitzpatrick—what . . . have . . . you . . . *done?*"

Well, Ethan's transgression didn't go over too well with his in-laws, either—at first. The last time a Soderstrom voted for a Democrat was for Grover Cleveland. And it wouldn't be easy to change. But Feldon resolved he'd just have to swallow hard and support the boy, quietly, despite the shame, because he was *family* now. Just forgive and chalk it up to him being a convert and all, since Feldon now had the welfare of a new grandchild to think about. And the grandchild was *good* news. And they all thought about that *good* news every day.

Laycee and Ethan started thinking about names. They didn't ask VerJean's opinion on the subject, so she had to *volunteer* it. VerJean thinks it's a nice thing to name a child after *both* of the parents. She said it could be Laythan if it was a boy, or Elayce if it was a girl. (One of the drawbacks of being married and living with your parents is you have to put up with stuff like that.) Laycee and Ethan agreed that Laycee will have the final say if it turns out to be a girl, and Ethan will choose the name if the baby is a boy. And they've both been going through lots of names and thinking about 'em. And *that* is good news.

And that's how things were through the spring and the summer and into the fall. Ethan didn't campaign for the office. He mostly kept a low profile, since he was unopposed.

But Brother Rasmussen watched the calendar wind down toward the first Tuesday in November like it would be the end of the world.

Three weeks ago, he couldn't take it any longer, and he paid a visit to Belwin Norby, the retiring county surveyor. Brother Rasmussen got out the handkerchief, and he explained to Belwin how true and correct principles were hanging by a thread, and that the way for the adversary to triumph is for good men to do nothing—and if not him, *whom?* And if not now, *when?*

Belwin listened. He listened and he thought and he looked deep within his soul, his seventy-eight-year-old soul, and he decided he had one more term left in him. And he went down to the office of the weekly, and he took out an ad to declare his change of heart. And the next edition of *The Progress*—the one that came out two weeks ago—presented Belwin Norby as the incumbent Republican *write-in* candidate for Taylor County surveyor, seeking a tenth consecutive term.

There weren't nearly as many votes in Taylor County for the surveyor candidates as there were for Congress, because, I suppose, some straight-ticket voters simply missed the race. And with Ethan's name on the ballot in print, he probably benefited from some confusion. But in the end, as it says here:

> **County Surveyor: Ethan Fitzpatrick,**
> **Democrat, 53; Belwin Norby, write-in,**
> **1,269.**

So Belwin won. "And he *deserved* it," Brother Rasmussen said, in the conclusion to his sermon to the men at VarDell's. "It ended aright," he said. "*That's* the good news. But," he said, "I sorrow to think how the ballot was tarnished. And I am not guiltless in that thing." He took out the handkerchief for one more wipe.

"But this all goes to show," he said, "just goes to show as the Bible says, 'even the very elect' can be deceived. To be sure." And he blew his nose.

While Brother Rasmussen was preaching at VarDell's on Thursday, Ethan was up at the seminary. He still has *that* job. Just barely. His foolishness caused him a lot of grief. And he was up there alone and, I suppose, feeling pretty bad. But on the bright side, the baby is due any day. That's good news. And he was working out the special effect for his next lesson, which was Moses and the burning bush. Ethan had dug up a sagebrush. Soaked it in fire retardant for a week. Arvel Eckberg, the seminary principal, has put up with a lot from Ethan this year, and he told him he'd have to do this one outside. Ethan had been down to the junkyard, where he got Trulan to lend him a blow torch. And as he tested it out, the special effect looked pretty good!

Ethan went back inside the building to review the story of Moses and his call. He turned to Exodus 2, and he read a name he hadn't remembered—a name he thought he might just give their baby if it turns out to be a boy. The verses said Moses was content to live with the man who gave him his daughter to wife. *And she bore him a son.* And . . . *He called his name Gershom, for he said, "I have been a stranger in a strange land."*

Gershom. He could name his boy *Gershom.* Ethan's been thinking about it.

We just hope it's a girl.

Part of that story's in the hometown weekly, the good news newspaper that helps you remember who you are and where you're from.

IS PARLEY BURNING?

The hometown weekly just came in the mail. I love this paper! After all my years in the television news business, it's a reality check on what people like me do. And sometimes it puts us to shame. Like this week.

In *The Progress* this week is the other side of a story you may have seen last week on TV. The story happened last Wednesday—a week ago Wednesday, which was too late for last Thursday's edition of *The Progress*. But it's all here *this* week, on the front page above the fold. It's a reminder that there is more than one way to look at the world. And some ways may be better than others for keeping your balance, I would dare say.

It's not very often that *The Progress* in Parley Grove and KWOW-TV, Channel Eight Frenzied News in Salt Lake City, ever lead with the same story. In fact, this is the only time I've seen that happen. But here it is, in the weekly.

It's almost unheard of for *The Progress* and Channel Eight Frenzied News to even cover the same event. And Parley Grove hardly ever gets mentioned on TV. So I think a little explanation about how this happened is in order.

KWOW-TV did not set out to do a report from Parley Grove. One of its crews just stumbled onto something near there while driving by last week in their mini-satellite truck. They were on their way back to Salt Lake from a feature they'd done at Lake Powell—a live at Noon, and a taped report for Ten—on water-skiing squirrels.

They were taking the back road home, through Taylor County, when they came over the rise and saw billowing smoke and flames across the valley that looked like a fire line stretching for miles. Through the smoke you could hardly see the big white-washed letters on the hill, the *P* and the *G,* or the little town below, surrounded by poplar trees—all of them still bare, too early in the season for the leaves to be out.

Well, Channel Eight Frenzied News is nothing if it's not competitive. That *is* the name of the game. And since no other Salt Lake station had given live coverage to Lake Powell's International Water-Skiing Squirrel Competition, Hunter Rage—the reporter for Channel Eight Frenzied News—was sure she would have an exclusive on this story, too. It didn't take a rocket scientist to know that all the flames and smoke were *something*. And, as it happens, Hunter Rage is no rocket scientist!

Hunter Rage just came to Salt Lake four months ago from Florida. Fort Meyers was her last job, and Reno before that, and Altoona before *that*. Give her about two years and she'll be off to somewhere else, somewhere bigger still, working her way up that cutthroat ladder toward TV fame and glory.

It was close to four in the afternoon—a cool March afternoon—when Hunter and her photographer, Breed, drove over the rise.

"Mother of Pearl!" she said (or some exclamation to that effect). "We gotta get this on the air!"

She dialed the station on her cell phone. She dialed the number again. She dialed it three times. She just wouldn't believe Breed when he told her there was no cell coverage out there. He said what they ought to do was just shoot some tape once they got closer to the flames and she could find out what it was, and they could just drive the pictures up to the station for a story for the Ten. Breed's been at the station for three years now, and he did grow up in American Fork, so he might have better judgment about these things.

But Hunter said, "You're so totally nineties. Today, it's all about live. *Live*, Breed. Don't you get it? *Live*. This'll be a great live lead for the Five."

Breed said, "Well, how are you gonna get it to lead the Five if you can't even call the station?"

She said, "Pull over and stop. Put up the dish. We'll use the satellite phone."

In a situation like this, the reporter calls the shots, especially a reporter with the drive of Hunter Rage. She knows KWOW-TV Channel Eight Frenzied News is in a dogfight for fourth place in the ratings, and there's nothing like breaking mayhem and disaster, *live*, to hook the viewers. And she is *good* at live. This girl can ad lib on her feet in a breathless torrent of raw energy before ever getting to the who, what, when, where, or why—if, indeed, she ever *does*. Just give her a microphone—a mic and the camera— and Hunter Rage will whip some journalism on you 'til you're ready to beg her to stop.

So Breed pulled the truck over on the shoulder of the road and stopped. He set up the dish, and Hunter called in to the desk at KWOW-TV Channel Eight Frenzied News. She said, "I've got your new lead for the Five. It's breaking news. It's exclusive. All of podunk here is going up in flames. We'll have great pictures, and I'll do it live."

The managing editor said, "Mother of Pearl!" (or some equivalent expression). "Hurry and feed us some pictures we can turn around on tape, and we'll put you in headlines and take you off the top."

Hunter said, "That's a ten-four," which is something she learned to say in Altoona.

Breed had his camera set up on the tripod so he could zoom in tight on the smoke across the valley—thick white smoke rising in a narrow line running north to south, a line of smoke (with a few lingering flames) that made it almost impossible to see Parley Grove, just beyond. From the side of the highway there on the rise, they had a panorama of that wall of smoke, rising hundreds and hundreds of feet, almost straight up, because there was hardly any wind.

Hunter said to Breed, "Can you feed the tape? Do you have enough?" Breed said he'd really like to drive in closer to see what was actually burning. But Hunter said they should feed the tape first, and then try to get down closer to the fire line for the live standup position, if they had the time.

Breed popped the camera off the tripod to take it to the truck just as they heard a car coming up from behind them over the rise. Hunter stepped into the middle of the road and waved her arms over her head. This is a woman who would stand in the middle of the railroad tracks and wave down a speeding train. She grabbed Breed's mic and brought him along to interview the driver for his reaction to the smoke. She needed a soundbite from *somebody*.

In the car was a young family with three kids on their way home to Kaysville from Kanab. Well, Hunter worked 'em over—and she worked 'em over good!

Breed rewound the tape with the smoke and the interviews and got ready to bounce it off the satellite to the downlink at KWOW-TV. It was now 4:25—just thirty-five minutes to air. Hunter called the producer to give her some in-cues and out-cues. After dictating a few cues for the director to follow, she said, "Beyond that, we're going to wing it, so just stay with me."

Hunter told Breed to fold up the dish. They had just enough time to drive right up to the edge of the smoke, where she would do a dramatic live standup report.

It's a pressure business, this TV news. It's a deadline business. You're always fighting the clock. And you're always trying to stand out from everybody else.

It was a scramble to pack the gear, drive closer to the action, get everything out, and set it up all over again. And Breed got no help from Hunter Rage. She was pacing back and forth on the highway, rehearsing at full voice what she was going to say. To *see* her there, stepping in and out of the smoke, waving her arms and shouting her lines . . . it was not a bad impression of Lady Macbeth.

Breed dialed the control room on the satellite phone. Hunter put in her earpiece, smeared on some lip gloss, and checked herself in a pocket mirror.

From the control room in Salt Lake the director said, "Two minutes to air. I need a mic check from Hunter."

Hunter said, "Mic check. Mic check. One two three four five six seven eight nine ten. Mic check. Mic check. Mic check."

"Got it," the director said.

Then the director said, "One minute."

Well, that's the explanation of how this came about. I thought it would be helpful. Maybe you saw the story last week on KWOW-TV Channel Eight Frenzied News Live at Five. If you didn't see it, just read the transcript. . . .

[NEWS OPENING] (stirring headline music under–)

[Hunter Rage, live]: *Walls of flame threaten to engulf an entire Utah city. I'm Hunter Rage reporting live. I'll tell you where it is.*

[In studio, Anchor Brick Hudson]: *Could something in that apple pie prove fatal to your kids? It's every mother's worst nightmare.*

[Speaking over videotape, Anchor Brandi Chablis]: *Police pursue a fleeing felon in a dramatic high-speed chase from his meth lab to the freeway, leaving terror in their wake. And his ex-girlfriend was in the car giving birth to a baby! Stay tuned for an exclusive video.*

[Two-shot in studio, Anchor Brick Hudson]: *All those stories, plus: Is your house on a hidden earthquake fault? Experts say the shaker of the century could strike at any moment.*

[Continuing two-shot, Anchor Brandi Chablis]: *Channel Eight Frenzied News Live at Five is next!*

[Stirring music under–]

[Montage images of mayhem–]

[Announcer]: *This is Channel Eight Frenzied News Live at Five, with Brick Hudson and Brandi Chablis. Uncle Ned Fishburn has weather, and Bart Dakota has Sports.*

[Music reaches crescendo and fades–]

[Brick Hudson]: *Good afternoon everybody.* (Over shoulder appears graphic: "Flames of Doom.") *It's only March, but it's hotter than blazes in south central Utah tonight as a searing wall of fire marches toward the town of Parley Grove. Our very own Hunter Rage is live on the scene to bring you the exclusive story. Hunter, I thought the fire season didn't start for three months.*

[Live satellite, Hunter Rage]: *That's right, Brick, just as you said, fire season usually doesn't start until summer, three months from now. But take a look! What we have here, before your eyes, is a scene that looks like Armageddon.*

The tape Breed shot from the rise an hour earlier flashes on screen. It's a better picture than what they have live, because the flames are mostly out.

[Hunter Rage]: *This afternoon that wall of flame roared across this valley, consuming everything in its path—annihilating it, leaving only ashes and the thick, white smoke that I'm standing in right now. I can tell you, Brick and Brandi, this stuff is literally very hard to breathe. The smell of burning is all around me now at the present time. And even as we speak, I'm surrounded by places where the flames still linger and it's too hot to even step. Just imagine what a shock it was for people to stumble onto something as unexpected as this.*

That was a roll cue. And at this point, the director in the studio called for another piece of tape with part of the interview Hunter beat out of those poor people in the car.

[Man in car]: *Well, we seen it when we come up over the rise. And, I'm like, "Whoa!"*

[Woman in car]: *It looks kind of—scary, I guess you'd say?*

[Hunter Rage]: *Would you say you feared for your lives?*

[Woman in car]: *Well, I sure wouldn't want to go driving through something like that. That's for sure.*

[Hunter Rage]: *You surely wouldn't risk it with these beautiful children.*

[Woman in car]: *Well, no. I mean—I love my children . . . because . . . because . . . .* (Camera shot zooms in on woman's face. Her voice catches.) . . . *Because children are the most precious thing in our lives.*

The shot lingers. Woman in car seems to be at a loss for words.

[Hunter Rage]: *It sounds like you work hard to be a good mother.*

[Woman in car, eyes tearing now]: [Gasp] *I try.*

[Cut back to Hunter Rage, live]: *So, there you have it, Brick and Brandi, very emotional reaction to all this devastation that has wreaked havoc here in Taylor County, burning—it would appear—right up to the edge of the town of Parley Grove. Back to you.*

[In studio, Anchor Brick Hudson]: *Hunter, can you tell us the progress of any efforts to fight the fire?*

[Live on location, Hunter Rage]: *Well, Brick, I can tell you that no aerial tankers have arrived at this hour. And we see no sign of helicopters, and no emergency vehicles are in the present vicinity. We really just arrived on the scene ourselves only moments ago as the first TV crew, so the outcome of firefighting efforts remains to be seen.*

[In studio, Anchor Brick Hudson]: *Hunter, can you describe the situation in Parley Grove at the present time? It's not a very big place, but there are, I guess, uh, a few hundred people. They must be in a state of panic right now.*

[Live on location, Hunter Rage]: *Well, Brick, if not panic, possibly shock. I can only tell you that the situation in Parley Grove at this hour is now pending. As I said, we just arrived first on the scene to discover this fire wreaking havoc up and down the valley almost as far and wide as the eye can see, and from here, with the smoke, you can't see much at all, so the situation in Parley Grove is undetermined at this time. Communication between our location and the town is totally nonexistent right now as we speak. And as soon as we finish here, we will immediately try to get to the town, if we can make it through the fire lines.*

So, to recap, Brick and Brandi, fire wreaks havoc near the town of Parley Grove. We are awaiting word of possible casualties and we have no damage estimates as of yet. But from the looks of things, it may be fair to say that any investigation into this blaze will continue.

[In studio, Anchor Brick Hudson]: *Incredible work, Hunter. You be careful, now.*

[Hunter Rage]: *Thanks, Brick.*

[In studio, Anchor Brandi Chablis]: *I'll say, Hunter, fantastic job.*

[Hunter Rage]: *Thanks.*

And that was what you saw on KWOW-TV, Channel Eight Frenzied News Live at Five.

I probably should not comment on my TV colleagues' work. So I won't. Let me simply ask you to read the version of the same story that appeared in *The Progress* this Thursday. The headline:

PARLEY GROVE SEEN ON TV
SPECIAL TO *THE PROGRESS*

Just below that was a three-column publicity head shot of Hunter Rage.

Prominently featured last week on widely viewed broadcasts of KWOW- TV Channel Eight Frenzied News in

Salt Lake City was our own town of Parley Grove.

Salt Lake City is the 36th largest TV market in the entire United States. Parley Grove Mayor Naff Dilson believes this was the first time Parley Grove has been featured on TV since 1989. That was when our fair city got left off the new state highway map, which was the result of a mistake.

"At least this time, the news knew where to find us," commented Mayor Dilson. "Maybe that's progress, I guess."

Making the report, which was broadcast live, was noted TV personality Hunter Rage. She has a wide range of experience, having appeared on television not only in Salt Lake City, but also in Fort Meyers, Florida; Reno, Nevada; and Altoona, Pennsylvania.

"This is my first visit to Parley Grove," said Miss Rage. "I hope someday I can return."

Following her live report, Hunter Rage signed autographs at the ChatNChew Cafe and met with local residents. Some had driven out from town to meet her on location where she performed her "live shot," as they call it in TV lingo. KWOW-TV is a network affiliate, which means the footage of Parley Grove could be picked up by other stations across the country or even around the world, Miss Rage said.

Imagine the surprise of Parley Grovers who were watching KWOW-TV Channel Eight's Frenzied News Live at Five when they saw our town, live, in the background on her report!

"We just couldn't hardly believe it," said Marvadel Ovard, who was watching at the time. "It almost makes us famous."

The occasion for Miss Rage's report was Norbert Egbert's annual ditch bank cleanup that he does for farmers every spring.

"If I'd of known people would be that interested in burning ditch banks, I could of sold tickets and charged admission!" Norbert stated. "But it's just good to see we're back on the map. Maybe it'll help get us some development in this town," Norbert added.

Clester Holdaway, owner of the Parley Rest Motel, said if Parley Grove's new notoriety succeeds in generating more tourism, he is ready. "We've got eight rooms and a family unit with a kitchenette—some utensils included," Holdaway said. "We could handle double the bookings, no problem at all."

Brother Rasmussen told *The Progress,* "Although I did not view the program and do not ordinarily watch TV in our home, it is destiny, I believe, that this place shall become known far and wide. And it may be for purposes we do not yet fully understand," he opined.

RoWayne Thackerall said she approached Miss Rage about filming a special on the Parley Creek Cloggers, and the charming celebrity promised she would consider it.

It was said by all who met Hunter Rage that she is as pretty in person as she is on the screen. Mayor Dilson said he will present Miss Rage with a key to the city, as soon as he gets one made.

Miss Rage spent nearly an hour with admiring fans at the ChatNChew Cafe, and a good time was had by all.

Which goes to show, if you want some good news for a change, you just need to put the right slant on it.

That's the *positive* version of the story from the hometown weekly, the good news newspaper that helps you remember who you are and where you're from.

ABOUT THE AUTHOR

Bruce Lindsay is the senior news anchor at KSL Television in Salt Lake City.

He got an early start in both broadcasting and hometown news as a college student.

When not in class, he was producing TV stories about ordinary people in small towns far off the main road.

Lindsay received a degree in Communications from Brigham Young University and an MBA from the University of Utah.

He is married to Shari Anderson Lindsay, the light of his life. They are the parents of four beautiful daughters and two handsome sons.

Photo courtesy of KSL